The Spellcoats

Now the thing that finally decided us to leave was this. It was around dawn, though there was no light coming in round the shutters as yet. My neck ached down one side and my mouth tasted bad. The fire was very low, but I could see Duck rolling and stirring in front of it. Hern was sitting on the table.

"The floor's all wet," he said.

I put my hand on the hearthrug to move, and it was like a marsh. "Ugh!" I said. It is a noise there is no word for.

At that, the door to the bedroom swung open and there was Gull in his nightshirt, feeling at the frame of the door as he had done before. I heard his feet splash in the water on the floor. "Is it time?" Gull asked.

Diana Wynne Jones

THE SPELLCOATS

A Beech Tree Paperback Book · New York

The Library of Congress has cataloged the Greenwillow Books
edition of *The Spellcoats* as follows:
Jones, Diana Wynne.
The spellcoats / by Diana Wynne Jones.
p.   cm. — (The Dalemark quartet ; bk. no. 3)
Summary: Tanaqui discovers she has the only means to conquer
the evil Kankredin who threatens her own people and the
Heathens who have invaded prehistoric Dalemark.
ISBN 0-688-13362-2 (rte.)   ISBN 0-688-13401-7 (pbk.)
[1. Fantasy.]   I. Title.   II. Series: Jones, Diana Wynne.
Dalemark quartet ; bk. 3.
PZ7.J684Sp   1995
[Fic]—dc20   94-1507   CIP   AC

First Beech Tree Edition, 1995
1   3   5   7   9   10   8   6   4   2

For my sister Ursula

CONTENTS

PART ONE

The
First Coat

1

I WANT TO TELL of our journey down the River. We
are five. The eldest is my sister Robin. Next is my
brother Gull, and then my brother Hern. I come
fourth, and I am called Tanaqui, which is a name from
the scented rushes that line the River. This makes me
the odd one out in names, because my youngest
brother is Mallard—only we always call him Duck.
We are the children of Closti the Clam, and we lived
all our lives in the village of Shelling, where a stream
comes down to join the River, giving plentiful fishing
and rich pasture.

This makes Shelling sound a good place, but it is
not. It is small and lonely, and the people here are dark
and unpleasant, not excepting my aunt Zara. They

worship the River as a god. We know that is wrong. The only gods are the Undying.

Last year, just before the autumn floods, strangers came to Shelling from over the hills, carrying bundles and saying that our land had been invaded by strange and savage Heathens, who were driving all our people out. Hern, Duck, and I went and stared at them. We had not known that we had any land except the country round Shelling. But Gull says the land is very large, and the River only the center part of it; there have been times when Gull has said quite reasonable things.

The strangers were not very interesting. They were just like Shelling people, only rather more worried. They hired my father to ferry them over the River, which is wide here, and then went on their way beyond this old mill on the far side. But, a week after them, people arrived on horseback: very stern smart men wrapped in scarlet rugcoats, with steel clothes under that. And these men said they were messengers from the King. They carried a golden stork wearing a crown on a stick to prove it. When my father saw the stork, he said they were indeed from the King.

We stared at these men far longer than at the others. Even Robin, who was very shy then, left the baking and came and stood beside us with her arms all floury. The smart men riding past all smiled at her, and one winked and said, "Hallo, sweetheart." Robin went very pink, but she did not go away as she used to when the Shelling boys called such things.

It seemed these messengers had come collecting men to fight the Heathens. They stayed one night, during which time they had all the men and boys walk before them and told the ones who were fit that they must prepare to come to the wars. It seems they had the right. It seems the King has this right. I was very surprised because I had not known we had a King over us before. Everyone laughed. Hern pretended to laugh at me with Robin and Gull and my father, but he confessed afterward that he had thought Kings were of the Undying, and not really of this world at all. We agreed that a King was a better thing to have over us than Zwitt, the Shelling headman. Zwitt is an old misery, and his mouth is all rounded from saying no.

The messengers told Zwitt he must go to war, and for once he could not say no. But they also told Aunt Zara's husband, Kestrel, that he must go. Kestrel is an old man. My father said this must mean that the King's case was desperate indeed. It made Hern feverishly hopeful. He said if they took Kestrel, they would surely take boys of Hern's age, too. Gull said nothing. He just smiled. Altogether Gull was odious that evening.

Hern crept secretly away and prayed to our Undying, in their three niches by the hearth. He prayed to them to make him fit to go to war and swore that he would free the land from the Heathen if they did. I know this because I heard him. I was coming to pray, too. I must say I was surprised at Hern. He usually scoffs at our Undying, because they are not real and reasonable like the rest of life. It shows how much he wanted to go to war.

When Hern had gone, I knelt and implored our Undying to turn me into a boy so that I could fight the Heathen. I am as tall as Hern, and wiry, although Hern beats me when we fight. Robin sighs and calls me boyish, mostly because my hair is a bush. I prayed very deeply to the Undying. I swore, like Hern, that I would free the land from the Heathen if they made me a boy. They did not answer me. I am still a girl.

Then it was time for my father, Gull, and Hern to walk before the King's men. They chose my father at once. And they dismissed Hern at once, saying he was too skinny and young. But Gull has always been tall and sturdy for his age. They told Gull he could go to war if he wished and if my father agreed, but they would not press him. They were fair men. Of course Gull wished to go to war. My father, now he knew he had a choice, was not altogether willing to let Gull go, but he thought of poor old Uncle Kestrel, and he told Gull he could go, provided he stayed close to Uncle Kestrel. Gull came home delighted and boasted all evening. I told you he was odious then. Hern came home trying not to cry.

In the morning the messengers went to the next village to choose men there, giving the men of Shelling a week to prepare themselves. For that week we were weaving, baking, hammering, and mending for dear life, getting Gull and my father ready. Hern was like a broody hen the whole time. He made Duck miserable, too. Robin says I was as bad, but I deny it. I had found a way to comfort myself by pretending I was a very fierce and warlike person called Tanaqui the Terror of the Heathen. When the messengers came back to Shelling, I pretended they would hear of this person and send Zwitt to fetch her to lead our land to war. I told it to our Undying, to make it seem more true. I wish now that I had not done that. Sometimes I think this is what brought such troubles on us. You should not speak falsehoods to the Undying.

Robin says we all got worse, Hern, Duck, and I, every time Aunt Zara came in. She kept coming and thanking my father for taking Gull to look after Kestrel, and she kept promising she would look after us all when they were away. It was all words. She never came near us. But I think my father believed her, and it took a weight off his mind.

After a week the messengers came back, bringing some hundreds of men with them. That night, before they were to leave, my father and Gull naturally prayed to the Undying for safety.

Robin said anxiously, "I'd be happier if you took one of them with you."

"They belong by this hearth," said my father. He would not say any more about it. "Hern," he said. "Come here."

Hern would not come at first, but my father dragged him by one arm over to the Undying. "Now put your hand on the One," he said, "and swear that you will stay with Duck and the girls and not try to follow us to war."

Hern was red in the face, and I could see he was very angry, but he swore. That is my father all over. He never said much—they called him the Clam with good reason—but he saw what was in people's minds. After Hern had sworn, Father looked at Duck and me. "Do I need to make you two swear as well?"

We said no. Duck meant it. He had grown scared that week while he was sharpening my father's weapons. I was still fancying to myself that the messengers would send Zwitt in the morning to fetch Tanaqui the Terror.

So much for my fancies! Next morning all the men from Shelling marched away except Zwitt. Zwitt— would you believe this!—fell ill and could not go. What kind of illness is it that has a man in a fever in the morning and out fishing in the afternoon? Hern says it is a very rare and uncommon disease called cowardice.

We went with the rest of Shelling to wave the army off. I do not think I like armies. They are about five hundred men, which is quite a large crowd of people, dressed in all sorts of old tough rugcoats, and some in fur or leather, so that they look as brown and scaly as River mud. Each of these people carries bags and weapons and scythes and pitchforks, all in different ways, so that the army looks like an untidy pincushion or a patch of dead grass. There is a King's man riding at the side, shouting, "All in line there! *Left*, right, left, right!" The crowd of people do as he says, not willingly, not fast, so that the army flows off like the River, brown, sluggish, and all one piece. As if people could become like water, all one thing! We could hardly distinguish Father or Gull, though we looked hard. They had become all one with the rest. And as the army flows off, it leaves a dull noise, dust in the air, and a smell of too many men, which is not pleasing. It made me feel sick. Robin was white. Duck said, "Let's go home." As for Hern, I truly think he lost all desire to go to war that morning, just as I did.

Zwitt called everyone together and said the war would not last long. He said confidently that the King would soon beat the Heathens. I should not have believed a bad man like Zwitt. It was many months before we had news.

Life in Shelling went on, but it was small, quiet, and empty. The autumn floods came late. They were less than usual and smelled bad. Everyone agreed that the River was angry because of the Heathens—and they began saying other things, too, that we did not hear until later. The floods did not bring as much driftwood as usual, but they washed up strange fish, which nobody liked to eat.

Though Aunt Zara did nothing to help the four of us, we did not go short. We had vegetables from the garden, and the flour was milled from our field. Duck and Hern always catch fish. Duck can find clams by instinct, too, I think. The hens were laying well, even in the winter, and we had the cow for milk. Money for other things was scarce, because we had just laid in a great deal of wool when Zwitt's flock was sheared, before the Heathens came. This I combed and spun and dyed in the ways that my mother had taught Robin and my father, and they have taught me. My mother taught Robin to weave. I was too young to learn when she died, but Robin taught me, and now I do it better than she does. It is that same wool I am using now to weave our story. We did not find much market for my weaving in Shelling that winter. A number of children needed winter rugcoats. But my main—and my best—work is always for weddings. The girls' families buy my finest rugcoats, with stories and poems in them, to give to the boy they are going to marry. But there were no weddings, with the men all gone. And after we went across the River, no one wanted any of my weaving.

The floods had left us no driftwood to speak of, so we rowed across the River when the leaves started falling to cut wood from the forest on the other side. No one else in Shelling crosses the River. I asked Aunt Zara why once, and she said that the old mill was cursed by the River, and the forest round it, and that they were haunted by a cursed spirit in the shape of a woman. That was why the new mill was built, up along the stream. When I told my father what Aunt Zara said, he laughed and told me not to listen to nonsense. It is quite a pleasure to me to sit weaving in this same old mill, with this same cursed forest round me, at this very moment, and take no harm. There's for you, Aunt Zara!

The day we cut wood, the light was rich with the end of autumn. It was like a holiday. We broke the stillness of the trees by running about shouting, catching falling leaves, and playing Tig. I do not think there were any spirits who minded, in spite of what Robin said. And she ran about and shouted with us, anyway. She was far more as I remember her, that day, before she grew up and got all shy and responsible. We had lunch sitting on the grass by the old millpool, and after that we cut wood. When the River was pale in the dusk, we rowed back over, with wood heaped in such a stack that the boat was right down in the water and we had to sit still for fear of being swamped. My hair was like a real bush, full of twigs and leaves. I was really happy.

Next day Zwitt and some of the old people came to us with sour faces. They said we were not to pasture our cow with the others in future. "We do not give grazing rights to godless people," Zwitt said.

"Who's godless?" Duck said.

"The River has forbidden people to cross to the mill," Zwitt said. "And you were all there all yesterday. The River would punish you worse than this if you were older."

"It's not the River punishing us. It's you," said Duck.

Hern said, "You didn't punish my father for ferrying the strangers over there."

"Who told you we were there?" I said.

"Zara told me," said Zwitt. "And you watch how you speak to me, now your father's away. I won't stand for rudeness."

Robin wrung her hands when they had gone. It was her latest ladylike habit, but it meant she was really upset. "Oh dear! Perhaps the spirits over there are angry. Do you think we did offend the River?"

We were not having that. We respect the River, of course, but it is not one of the Undying, and we do not believe in spirits flocking around being angry at everything, the way Zwitt does. I told Robin she was growing up as joyless as Zwitt. Hern said it did not make sense to talk of a river's being offended.

"And if it is, *it* ought to punish us, not Zwitt," said Duck.

"I only meant that it *could* be offended," Robin said.

When we had finished arguing, Hern said, "It sounds as if Zwitt was afraid of my father."

"I wish he'd come back!" I said.

But the months passed and no one came back. Meanwhile, we were forced to move our cow to the edge of the River, just beside our house. We think that was why she never caught the cattle plague all the other cows got. Hern is sure it was. A great deal of mist came off the River that winter and hung about the pasture. Of course our cow was grazing peacefully in the mist most of the time, on the Riverbank, but the other people said it was the mist that brought the disease. When some cows died, and ours had never coughed once, they began giving us very black looks.

Hern was furious. He called them narrow-minded fools. Hern believes there are reasons for everything, and that curses and bad luck and spirits and gods do not make real reasons. "And why is it *our* fault their wretched cows die?" he demanded. "Because *we* offended the River, if you please! In that case, why is our cow all right?"

Robin tried to pacify him. "Hern, dear, don't you think it could be our Undying looking after us?"

"Oh—running river-stinks!" said Hern, and flounced out to the woodshed with such a look of scorn that Robin went into the scullery to cry—she cries a lot—and I stood on the hearth wondering whether to cry, too. I do not cry much, so I talked to Duck instead. It is no good talking to Robin, and Hern is so *reasonable*. Duck is young, but he has a lot of sense.

"Hern doesn't believe in the Undying," Duck said. "It's because they're not reasonable."

"Then why didn't he run away after the army?" I said. "He didn't, because he'd sworn on the Undying."

"He didn't because he saw the army," said Duck. "Anyway, the Undying *aren't* reasonable."

"Don't you believe in them either?" I said. I was truly shocked. Hern is one thing, but Duck is younger than me. Besides, we were standing right beside the Undying in their niches, and they must have heard Duck.

Duck turned to look at them. "You don't have to believe in things because they're reasonable," he said. "Anyway, I like them."

We both looked quite lovingly at our three Undying. Two of them are old. They have been in my father's family for generations. I can remember lying in my cradle by the fire, looking up at them. Hern says I could not possibly remember, but that is Hern all over. I do remember. The Young One has a face that seems to smile in the firelight, though by daylight you can hardly see his face at all. He is carved of a rosy kind of stone that has worn very badly. You can just see that he is playing a flute, but not much else. The One is even older. It is hard to see what he is really like at all, except that he is a head taller than the Young One. The stone he is made of generally looks rather dark, with glistening flecks in it, but he changes every year when he has been in his fire. The Lady is made of hard, grainy wood. When my father first carved her, just after Duck was born, I remember she was light-colored like the tops of mushrooms, but she has darkened over the years, and now she is brown as a chestnut. She has a beautiful, kind face.

Duck chuckled. "They're a lot nicer than Uncle Kestrel's lump of wood."

I laughed, too. Everyone in Shelling has such awful Undying. Most of them are supposed to be the River. Uncle Kestrel has a piece of driftwood that his father caught in his net one day. It looks like a man with one leg and unequal arms—you know how driftwood does—and he never lets it out of his sight. He took it to the war with him.

I remember this particularly. It was in the first part of the year after the shortest day, and there was a hard frost that night. It was the only frost that winter. I was cold. Right in the middle of the night I woke up out of a dream, freezing. In my dream my father was somewhere in the distance, trying to tell me something. "Wake up, Tanaqui," he said, "and listen carefully." But that was all he said, because I did wake up. It took hours to get back to sleep. I had to get in beside Robin in the end, I was so cold.

From what Uncle Kestrel said, I think that was the night my father died. It is hard to be sure, but I think so. I do not want to weave of this.

Before that came the terrible illness. Almost everyone in Shelling got it, and some of the smaller children died. The River smelled very bad. Even Hern admitted that this disease might have come from the River. It was much warmer than it should be for the time of year, and the River was very low and stagnant—a queer light greenish color—and we could not get the smell out of our house. Robin burned cloves on the edge of the hearth to hide it. We all had the disease, but not badly. When we were better, Robin and I went round to see if Aunt Zara was ill, too. We had not seen her in her garden for days.

She was ill, but she would not let us into her house. "Keep away from me!" she screamed through the door. "I'm not having either of you near me!"

Robin was very patient, because Aunt Zara was ill. "Now, Aunt, don't be so silly," she said. "Why won't you let us in?"

"Just look at yourselves!" screamed my aunt.

Robin and I stared at one another in great surprise. Robin had been very particular about our appearance, partly because she has grown fussy now she is old and partly to please Aunt Zara, who is even fussier. We both had our new winter rugcoats on, with bands of scarlet saying "Fight for the King," which I had woven to remind us of the King's messengers. The rest was a pattern of good browns and blue, which suit us both. My head was still sore from Robin's combing, so I knew my hair was neat and not the usual white bush. Robin's hair is silkier than mine, though just as curly. She had striven with it and put it into neat plaits, like a yellow rope on each shoulder. We could not see what was wrong with us.

While we looked, my aunt kept screaming. "I'm not going to have anything to do with you! I disown you! You're none of my flesh and blood!"

"Aunt Zara," Robin said, reasonably, "our father is your brother."

"I hate him, too!" screamed my aunt. "He brought you down on us! I'm not having the rest of Shelling saying it's my fault. Get away from my house!"

I saw Robin's face go red, then white. Her chin was a hard shape. "Come along, Tanaqui," she said. "We'll go back home." And she went, with me trotting to keep up. I looked at her as I trotted, expecting her to be crying, but she was not. She did not speak about Aunt Zara again. I spoke, but only a little, when Hern asked me what had happened.

"She's a selfish old hag, anyway," Hern said.

Aunt Zara recovered from the sickness, but she never came near us, and we did not go near her.

It was a long winter. The Spring floods were late in coming. We were longing for them, to wash away the smell from the River. I was longing for them in a special way. After my dream I was very anxious for my father, but I hid my worry in a new fancy: that he would come home in floodtime, before the One had to go in his fire, and everything would be all right. Instead no floods came, but at last men began to come back to Shelling from the wars. That was a time I do not want to tell about. Only half came back who had set out, weary and thin. My father and Gull were not among them, and no one would speak to us. Everyone looked at us grimly.

"What are we supposed to have done *now*?" Hern demanded.

:⊩ 2 ⊩:

UNCLE KESTREL CAME home among the last. He came to our house first, leading Gull. We were frightened when we looked at them. None of us could behave as if we were glad, though Robin tried. Uncle Kestrel had turned into a real old man. His head nodded, and his hands shook, and his face was covered with scraggly white bristle. Gull was inches taller. I knew it must be Gull because of his fair hair and the rugcoat I had woven for him last autumn, though that was shiny with grease and almost in rags, but I would not have known him otherwise.

"Be easy on him," Uncle Kestrel said when Robin threw her arms round Gull. Gull hardly moved. "He's had a bad time. It was the Heathens in the Black

Mountains did it. We were all in the siege there, and the slaughter."

Gull did not show he had heard. His face was empty. Robin led him to a seat, where he sat and stared. Duck, Hern, and I stood in a row looking at him. Only Robin remembered to ask Uncle Kestrel to come in. She bustled about for cake and drinks, and dug the three of us in our backs to make us help her. Duck fetched the cups. I pulled myself together and got out our best plum preserves, but my face kept turning to Gull, sitting staring, and then to Uncle Kestrel, so old. Hern just stood there staring at Gull as hard as Gull stared into space.

Uncle Kestrel is a very direct person. "Well," he said as soon as he was sitting down, "your father's dead, I'm afraid. Out on the plains, a long way from here."

We were all expecting that. None of us, not even Robin, cried. We just went pale and slow, and sat down without wanting to eat to hear what Uncle Kestrel had to tell.

Uncle Kestrel was glad of the good food. He beamed at Robin and ate a great deal. Whatever war had done to Gull, Uncle Kestrel came out of it completely natural. In the most natural way he broke off a big lump of cake, put it in Gull's hand, and closed Gull's fingers round it. "Here you are. Eat it, boy." Gull obediently ate the cake without looking at it—without looking at anything. "You'll find you have to do that," Uncle

Kestrel explained to us. "He'll drink the same way. Now, to the sad news."

He told us how Father had died of wounds in the middle of winter, a long way off. I think, from the way he said it, that my father had dragged himself along pretending to be well for Gull's sake, because Gull had needed looking after even then. The fighting had been terrible. Our people were not used to it, and few of them had real weapons. The Heathen had good weapons, spears, and bows that could send an iron bolt through two men at once. "Besides being trained from their cradles to fight like devils," Uncle Kestrel said. "And they have enchanters in their midst, who conquer us with spells. They can draw the strength from you like sucking an egg."

Hern stared. "Piffle."

"You haven't seen them, lad," said Uncle Kestrel. "I have. You know them by their long coats. They've set their spells on the very River himself, knowing him to be our strength and our lifeblood. Take a look outside, if you don't believe me. Have you ever known him that color and smelling like he does?"

"No," Hern admitted.

"So, by fair means and foul," Uncle Kestrel said, "the Heathen have beaten us. They've brought their women and their children, and they mean to stay. The land is full of them. Our King is in hiding, bless him."

"What will we all do?" Duck asked in an awed whisper.

"Run away to the mountains, I suppose," said Uncle

Kestrel. He looked worn out at the idea. "I've run from them for months now. But you five might stay if you wished, I think. This is a funny thing—" He glanced at Gull and began to whisper. I do not think Gull was listening, but it was so hard to tell. "The Heathen look almost like you do—the fair hair. He's had a deal to bear—Gull—from our side saying he was a Heathen changeling and bringing bad luck, and from the time the Heathen took him, thinking he was one of them." We all stared at Gull. "Be easy on him," said Uncle Kestrel. "As you see, they gave him back—this was in the Black Mountains—but he was not himself after that. Our men said he carried the Heathen's spells, and they might have killed him but for your father."

"How awful!" Robin said in a very high voice, like a sneeze or an explosion.

"True," said Uncle Kestrel. "But we had our good times." Then for quite a while he sat and told us jokes about people we did not know and things we did not understand, to do with the fighting. I am sure he meant to cheer us up. "That's what kept me sane, seeing the jokes," he said. "Now I suppose I'd better be off to see Zara." He got up and limped away. He did not behave much as if he was looking forward to seeing my aunt. Nor would I, in his shoes.

Robin cleared the cups away. She kept looking at Gull, and Gull just sat. "I don't know what to do with him," she whispered to me.

I went away outside, in spite of the smell from the River. I was hoping to be able to cry. But Hern was sitting in the boat, on the mud below the Riverbank, and he was crying.

"Just think of Gull like that!" he said to me. "He'd be better dead. I wish I'd gone after the army."

"What good would it have done?" I said.

"Don't you see!" Hern jumped up, so that the boat squelched about. "Gull had nobody to talk to. That's why he got like that. Why was I such a coward?"

"You swore to the Undying," I reminded him.

"Oh that!" said Hern. He was very fierce and contemptuous. The boat kept squelching. "*And* I swore to fight the Heathen. I could swear to a million things, and it wouldn't do any good. I just wish—"

"Stand still," I said. It suddenly seemed to me that it was not only Hern's angry movements that were making the squelching round the boat. Hern knew, too. He stood bolt upright with his face all tear-stained, staring at me. We felt the small shiver run along the banks of the River. The mud clucked, quietly, and a little soft lapping ran through the low green water. There were yards of bare mud on both sides of the River, but in a way that I do not know how to describe, it looked different to us. The trees on the other bank were stirring and lifting and expecting something.

"The floods are coming down," said Hern.

If you are born by the River, you know its ways. "Yes," I said, "and they're going to be huge this time."

Before we could say more, the back door crashed open, and Gull came out. He came out stumbling, feeling both sides of the door and not seeming to know quite where he was.

"The River," he said. "I felt the River." He stumbled over to the bank. I put out both hands to catch him because it looked as if he were going to walk right over the edge. But he stopped on the bank and swayed about a little. "I can hear it," he said. "I've dreamed about it. The floods are coming." He began to cry, like Robin sometimes does, without making a sound. Tears rolled down his face.

I looked at Hern, and Hern looked at me, and we did not know what to do. Robin settled it by racing out of the back door and grabbing Gull in both arms. She hauled him away inside, saying, "I'm going to put him to bed. It's frightening."

"The floods are coming down," I said.

"I know," Robin called over her shoulder. "I can feel them. I'll send Duck out." She pushed Gull through the door and slammed it.

Hern and I pulled the boat up. It was horribly hard work because it was stuck a long way down in the mud. Luckily Hern is far stronger than he looks. We got it up over the edge of the bank in the end. By that time the sick green water was racing in swelling snatches, some of them so high that they slopped into the grooves the boat had left.

"I think this is going to be the highest ever," Hern said. "I don't think we should leave it here, do you?"

"No," I said. "We'd better get it into the woodshed."

The woodshed is a room that joins the house, and the house is on the rising ground beyond the bank. Hern groaned, but he agreed with me. We got three of our last remaining logs to make rollers, and we rolled that heavy boat uphill, just the two of us. We had it at the woodshed when the woodshed door opened and Duck came out.

"You did arrive quickly!" I said.

"Sorry," said Duck. "We've been putting Gull to bed. He went straight to sleep. It's awful having him like this. I think there's nothing inside him!" Then Duck began to cry. Hern's arm tangled with mine as we both tried to get them round Duck.

"He'll get better," I said.

"Sleep will do him good," Hern said. I think we were talking to ourselves as much as to Duck.

"Gull's head of the family now," Duck said, and he howled. I envy both boys for being able to howl.

Hern said, "Stop it, Duck. There's the biggest ever flood coming down. We've got to get things inside." The River was hissing by then, *swish* and *swish*, as it began to spread and fill. The bad smell of winter was mixed with a new damp smell, which was better. I could feel the ground shaking under us, because of the weight of water in the distance.

"I can smell it," said Duck. "But I knew there was time to be miserable. I'll stop now." And he did stop, though he sniffed for the next hour.

We jammed the boat into the woodshed. I said we ought to bring the hens in there, too. Hens are funny things. They seem so stupid, yet I swear our hens knew about the floods. When we looked for them, they had all gone through the hedge to the higher ground above Aunt Zara's house and we could not get them back. They would not even come for corn. Nor would the cow go into the garden at first. Usually her one thought was to get in there and eat our cabbages. We pushed and pulled and prodded her, because we were sure she was not safe on the Riverbank, and tethered her where she could eat the weeds in the vegetable patch.

"She'll eat those cabbages somehow," said Duck. "Look at her looking at them."

We were pulling up all the cabbages near her when Robin came out. "Oh good," she said. "Pull enough for at least a week. I think the floods will be right up here by tomorrow. They feel enormous."

We ran around picking cabbages and onions and the last of the carrots and dumped them on the floor of the scullery.

"No," said Robin. "Up on the shelves. The water's coming in here."

She is the eldest, and she knows the River best. We did as she said. By this time it was getting dark. The River was making a long, rumbling sound. I watched it while Robin milked the cow. There was brown water as strong as the muscles in your leg piling through between the banks. The mud was covered already. I could see the line of yellow froth bubbles rising under the bank as I watched. The color of the water was yellower and yellower, as it always is in the floods, but it was a dark yellow, which is not usual. The air was full of the clean, earthy smell the floods bring. I thought it was stronger than usual, and sharper.

"There's been different weather up in the mountains where the River comes from, that's all," Hern said crossly. "Shall I wake Gull up and give him some milk?"

Gull was so fast asleep that we could not wake him. We left him and had supper ourselves. We felt strange—half excited because of the rumble of the water outside, half heavy with misery. We wanted sweet things to eat, but when we had them, we found we wanted salt. We were trying to make Robin cook some of the pickled trout when we heard an odd noise. We stopped talking and listened. At first there was only the River, booming and rushing. Then we heard someone scratching on the back door—scratching, not knocking.

"I'll go," said Hern, and he seized the carving knife on his way to the back door.

He opened it and there was Uncle Kestrel again, half in the dark, with his finger to his mouth for quiet. We twisted round in our seats and looked at him as he limped in. He had neatened himself up since he was last here, but he was still shaking.

"I thought you were the Heathen," Hern said.

"They'd be better company for you," said Uncle Kestrel. He smiled. He took a jam tart from Robin and said, "Thanks, my love," but that did not seem natural any longer. He was frightening. "Zwitt's been at my house," he said, "calling your family Heathen enchanters."

"We're not," said Duck. "Everyone knows we're not!"

"Do they?" asked Uncle Kestrel. He leaned forward over the table, so that the lamp caught a huge bent shadow of him and threw it trembling on the wall, across shelves and cups and plates. It looked so threatening with its long, wavering nose and chin that I think I watched it most of the time. It still scares me. "Do they?" said Uncle Kestrel. "There are men in Shelling who have seen Heathens with their own eyes, and who remember your mother—lovely girl she was, my Robin—looked just like the Heathen. Then Zwitt says you dealt ungodly with the River—"

"That's nonsense!" Hern said. He got angrier with everything Uncle Kestrel said. It was good of Uncle Kestrel not to take offense.

"You should have gone over to the old mill by night, lad," he said, "like I do when I go for mussels. And it's a pity neither you nor your cow got the sickness the River sent."

"But we all got it!" Robin protested. "Duck was sick all one night."

"But he lived when others his age died," said Uncle Kestrel. "There's no arguing with Zwitt, Robin, apple of my eye. He has the whole of Shelling behind him. If Duck died, they'd have thought up a reason for that. Don't you see? Do none of you see?"

The huge shadow shifted on the wall as he looked round the four of us. I saw that we seemed to be strangers in our own village, but I had known that before. So had Robin from the look of her. Duck looked quite blank. Hern almost shrieked, "Oh, yes, I see all right! Now my father's dead, Zwitt's not afraid of us anymore!"

The shadow shook its head and bent across two shelves. "But he is, lad. That's the trouble. They're frightened. The Heathen beat them. They want to blame someone. And spells have been cast by the Heathen. Hear the River now!"

We could all hear. I had never heard such rushing. The house shook with it.

Uncle Kestrel said softly, "He's coming down like that to fight the Heathen at the Rivermouth. That's where they set their spells, I heard."

"Oh!" said Hern. He was going to be rude.

"I understand," Duck said just then. "Zwitt wants to kill us, doesn't he?"

"Now, Duck!" Robin protested. "What a silly idea! As if—" She looked at Uncle Kestrel. "It's not true!"

The shadow on the wall shook. I thought it was laughing. I looked at Uncle Kestrel. He was serious—just shaking in that new old-man way of his. "It is true, my Robin," he said. "Zwitt was at my house to blame me cruelly for not killing young Gull while I had him. Gull carries the Heathen spells for you, it seems."

Nobody said anything except the River for a moment, and that rushed like thunder. In the midst of it Robin whispered, "Thank you, Uncle Kestrel."

"How are they going to kill us?" Hern said. "When?"

"They're meeting to decide that now," said Uncle Kestrel. "Some want to throw you to the River, I hear, but Zwitt favors cold steel. They often do who haven't seen it used." He stood up to go, and to my relief the huge shadow rose until it was too big for the wall to hold it. "I'll be off," he said, "now you understand. If Zara knew I was here, she'd turn me out."

"Where is Aunt Zara?" I asked.

"At the meeting," said Uncle Kestrel. He may have seen me look. As he limped to the door, he made me come with him while he explained. "Zara's not in an easy position. You must understand. She's afraid for her life of being called one of you. She had to go. It's different for me, you know." I still do not see why it should be different for Uncle Kestrel. Even Robin does not see.

I opened the door for him on such a blast of noise from the River that I put my hands to my ears. It was louder than the worst storm I have known. Yet there was barely any wind and only a few warm drops of rain. The noise was all the River. The lamplight showed black silk water and staring bubbles halfway to the back door.

Uncle Kestrel bawled something to me that I did not hear as he limped away. I slammed the door shut, and then Hern and I barricaded the doors and windows. We did not need to discuss it. We just ran about feverishly wedging the heaviest chairs against the doors and jamming benches and shelves across the shutters. We wedged the woodshed door by pushing the boat against it. We made rather a noise blocking the window just over Gull's bed, but Gull did not move.

All this while Duck was standing leaning his head against the niches of the Undying, and Robin was still sitting over supper. "I can't believe this!" she said. Another time we went by, she said, "We've only dear old Uncle Kestrel's word for it. He's not what he was. He may have misunderstood Zwitt. We've lived in Shelling all our lives. They wouldn't—"

"Yes, they would," Duck said from the niches. "We've got to leave here."

Robin wrung her hands. She will be ladylike. "But how can we leave, with the River in flood and Gull like this? Where should we go?"

I could see she had gone helpless. It annoys me when she does. "We can go away down the River and find somewhere better to live," I said. It was the most exciting thing I have ever said. I had always wanted to see the rest of the River.

"Yes. You can't pretend you've enjoyed living here this winter," Hern said. "Let's do that."

"But the Heathen!" Robin said, wringing away. I could have hit her.

"We look like the Heathen," I said. "Remember? We might as well make some use of it. We've suffered for it enough. I suppose Aunt Zara thought we were Heathen when she told us to go away."

"No," said Robin, being fair as well as helpless. It makes a maddening combination. "No, she couldn't have. She just meant we look different. We have yellow, wriggly hair, and everyone else in Shelling has straight black hair."

"Different is dead tonight," Hern said. Clever, clever.

"We've only Uncle Kestrel's word," said Robin again. "Besides, Gull's asleep."

So we sat about, with nothing decided. None of us went to bed. We could not have slept for the thousand noises of the flood, anyway. It made rillings and swirlings, rushings, gurglings, and babblings. Shortly there was rain going *blatter*, *blatter* on the roof and *spaah* when it came down the chimney and fell on the fire. Behind that the River bayed and roared and beat like a drum, until my ears were so bemused that I thought I heard shrill voices screaming out across the floods.

Then, around the middle of the night, I heard the real, desperate bellowing when our cow was swept away. Robin jumped up from the table, shouting for help.

Hern sat up sleepily. Duck rolled on the hearthrug. I was the most awake, so I scrambled up and helped Robin unblock the back door. It came open as soon as we lifted the latch, and a wave of yellow water piled in on us.

"Oh help!" said Robin. We heaved the door shut

somehow. It left a pool on the floor, and I could see water dripping in underneath it. "Try the woodshed!" said Robin.

We ran there, although I could tell that the cow's bellows were going away slantwise down the River now. Water was coming in steadily under the woodshed door. We pulled the boat back easily, because it was floating, but when we opened the door, the wave of water that came in was not quite so steep. Robin insisted that we could wade through the garden to the cow. We hauled up our clothes and splashed outside, trying to see and to balance and to hold skirts all at once. The rain was pouring down. That hissed, the River hissed and *gluck-glucked*, and the water swirled so that I half fell down against the woodshed. I knew it was hopeless. The cow was faint in the distance. But Robin managed to stagger a few yards on, calling to the cow, until even she was convinced there was nothing we could do.

"What shall we do for milk?" she said. "Poor cow!"

We could not shut the woodshed door. I tied the boat to one of the beams, and we waded back to the main room and shut that door. The woodshed is a step down. Soon water began to trickle under that door, like dark crawling fingers.

Robin sat by the hearth and I sat with her. "We shall drown if it comes much higher," she said.

"And Zwitt will say good riddance and the River punished us," I said. I sat leaning against Robin, watching water drip off my hair. Each drop had to turn twenty corners because my hair hangs in springs when it is wet. And I saw we would really have to leave now. We had no cow. We had no father to plow our field. Poor Gull could not do it, and Hern is not strong enough for that yet. We had no money to buy food instead, because no one would take my weaving, and even if we had, the people in Shelling probably would not sell us any. Then I remembered they were going to kill us, anyway. I thought I would cry. But no. I watched the firelight squeeze a smile out of the Young One's face, and Duck's mouth open and shut on the hearthrug, and the water from the woodshed trickle into a pool. Robin was soft and warm. She is maddening, but she does try.

"Robin," I said. "Did Mother look like us? Was she a Heathen?"

"I don't know," said Robin. "It's all vague. I think she had hair like ours, but I may be making it up. I don't remember. I don't even remember her teaching me to weave."

That surprises me still, Robin not remembering. She was nearly eight when our mother died. I was much younger when Robin taught me to weave, and I remember that perfectly. I can recall how Robin did not know the patterns for all the words, so that she and I together had to make quite a number up. I am not sure that anyone except my family will be able to read much of this, even of those who know how to read weaving. To everyone else, my story will look like a particularly fine and curious rugcoat. But it is for myself that I am weaving it. I shall understand our journey better when I have set it out. The difficulty is that I have to keep stopping because the clicking of my loom disturbs poor Robin.

:|| 3 ||:

Now THE THING that finally decided us to leave was this. It was around dawn, though there was no light coming in round the shutters as yet. My neck ached down one side, and my mouth tasted bad. The fire was very low, but I could see Duck rolling and stirring in front of it. Hern was sitting on the table.

"The floor's all wet," he said.

I put my hand on the hearthrug to move, and it was like a marsh. "Ugh!" I said. It is a noise there is no word for.

At that the door to the bedroom swung open, and there was Gull in his nightshirt, feeling at the frame of the door as he had done before. I heard his feet splash in the water on the floor. "Is it time?" Gull asked.

"Time for what?" said Hern.

"Time to leave," said Gull. "We have to go away down the River."

Robin, I swear, had been asleep up to then, but she was on her feet, splashing about, trying to soothe Gull back to bed before he had finished speaking. "Yes, yes. We're leaving," she said. "It's not quite time yet. Go back to bed till we're ready."

"You won't go without me?" Gull said as she shoved him back through the door.

"Of course not," said Robin. "But we haven't packed the boat yet. You rest while we do that, and I'll call you as soon as breakfast's ready."

While she put Gull back to bed, Hern and I splashed about in an angry sort of way, filling the lamp and lighting it again and putting the last logs on the fire. Duck woke up.

"Are we really leaving?" he said when Robin came back.

Hern and I thought Robin had just been soothing Gull, but she said, "I think we must. I think Gull knows best what the Undying want."

"You mean, the Undying told him we must go?" I said. Early though it was, my back pricked all the way down with awe. Usually I only get that in the evenings.

"Gull must have heard us talking," said Hern. "That explains it just as well. But I'm glad *something* made up your stupid minds for you. Let's get the boat loaded."

Then I did not want to go at all. Shelling was the place I knew. Everywhere beyond was an emptiness.

People came out of the emptiness and said things about Heathens with spells, the King, and war, but I did not believe in anywhere but Shelling really. I did not want to go into the nowhere beyond it. I think Hern felt the same at heart. We went slowly into the woodshed with the lamp, to push the boat out ready to load.

Water rolled in from the woodshed as soon as we opened the door. It came round our ankles like yellow silk, lazy and strong and smooth, and made ripples in the living room. Inside the shed the boat was floating level with the step. The lamp shone up from our startled reflections underneath it.

"You know," said Hern, "we can load it in here and just row out through the door."

I looked toward the door, dazzled by the lamp. I looked too low, where the land usually slopes toward the River, and I had one of those times when you do not know what you see. There was a long, bright streak, and in that streak, a smooth sliding. I thought I had been taken out of my head and put somewhere in a racing emptiness. There I was, upside down under my own feet—a bush of hair and staring eyes, wild and peculiar. I wonder if this is how Gull feels, I thought.

Duck did not like it either. "There's water high up, where the air usually is!" he said, and he waded over and tried to shut the door.

Hern was the only one of us who could shut the door against the force of the water. I always forget how strong Hern is. You would not think he was, to look at him. He is long and thin, with a stoop to his shoulders, very like the heron he was named for.

We argued a great deal over loading the boat and trailed up and down the ladder to the loft a great deal too often at first. Robin said we should take the apples. Hern said he hated last year's fruit. It was because none of us wanted to leave. Gradually, though, we grew excited, and the loading went quicker and quicker. Hern packed things in the lockers, shouting orders, and the rest of us ran to and fro remembering things. We packed so many pots and pans that there was nothing to cook breakfast in and almost nothing left to eat. We had to have bread and cheese.

Robin got Gull up and dressed him in warm clothes. The rest of us were in our thick old waterproof rugcoats, which I only make when they are truly needed, because it is double weave and takes weeks. My everyday skirt was soaked, and I did not want to spoil my good one. Besides, I had had enough of splashing about in a skirt in the night. I wore Hern's old clothes. I tried to persuade Robin to wear some of Gull's. A year ago she would have agreed. But now she insisted on being ladylike and wearing her awful old blue skirt— the one I made a mistake in, so that the pattern does not match.

The only warm rugcoat we could find which fitted Gull was my father's that my mother had woven him before they were married. My mother was mistress of weaving. The coat tells the story of Halian Tan Haleth, Lord of Mountain Rivers, and it is so beautiful that I had to look away when Robin led Gull to the table. The contrast between Mother's weaving and Robin's blue skirt was too painful.

It occurred to me while we were dressing Gull that there was not so much wrong with him as I had thought. He smiled once or twice and asked, quite reasonably, whether we had remembered fishing tackle and spare pegs for the mast. It was just that he stared so at nothing and did not seem to be able to dress himself. I wonder if he's blind, I thought. It did seem so.

I tested it at breakfast by pushing a slice of bread at Gull's face. Gull blinked and moved his head back from it. He did not tell me not to or ask what I thought I was doing, as Hern or Duck would have done, but he must have seen the bread. I put it in his hand, and he ate it, still staring.

"I tried that last night," Duck whispered. "He can see all right. It's not that."

We were sitting round the table with our feet hooked on the chair rungs because water was coming in from all the doors, even the front door, and most of the floor was a pool. There was a hill in the corner where my loom and spinning wheel stood, so that was dry, and so was the scullery, except for a dip in the middle. We laughed about it, but I did wish I could have taken my loom. The boat was so loaded by then that there was no point even suggesting it.

As I put the last slice of bread in Gull's hand, there was an explosion of sizzling steam from the hearth.

"Oh good gracious!" Robin shouted. She soaked us all by racing to the hearth. Water was spilling gently across the hearthstones and running in among the embers. Amid cloud upon cloud of steam, Robin snatched up the shovel and scooped up what was still alight. She turned round, coughing, waving one hand and holding up the red-hot shovelful. "The pot, the firepot, quickly! Oh, why do none of you ever help me?"

That fire has never been out in my lifetime. I could not think how we were to light it again if it did go out. At Robin's shriek, even Gull made a small bewildered movement. Hern splashed away for the big firepot we use in the boat, and I fetched the small one we take to the field. Duck took a breakfast cup and tried to scoop up more embers in that. He had only rescued half a cupful before the water swilled to the back of the fireplace and made it simply a black, steaming puddle.

"I think we've got just enough," Robin said hopefully, putting the lids on the pots.

Everything was telling us to leave, I thought as I waded with Hern to the woodshed to put the pots in the boat. The River had swung the outer door open again. It was light out there. Outside was nothing but yellow-brown River, streaming past so full and quiet that it seemed stealthy. There was no bank on the other side. The brown water ran between the tree trunks as strongly as it ran past the woodshed door. It was all so smooth and quiet that I did not realize at first how fast the River was flowing. Then a torn branch came past the door. And was gone. Just like that. I have never been so near thinking the River a god as then.

"I wonder if there's water all round the house," said Hern. We put the pots in the boat and waded back to see.

This was very foolish. It was as if, among all the other things, we had forgotten what Uncle Kestrel had told us. We climbed the slope beside my loom and took the plank off the shutters there. Luckily we only opened the shutter a crack. Outside was a tract of yellow, rushing water as wide as our garden, and not deep. On the farther edge of it, in a grim line, stood most of the men of Shelling. Zwitt was there, leaning on his sword, which looked new and clean because he had not been to the war. The swords of the others were notched and brown, and more frightening for that. I remember noticing, all the same, that behind them the yellow water had almost reached Aunt Zara's house. Where they were standing was a point of higher ground between the two houses.

"Look!" we called out, and Duck and Robin crowded to the open crack.

"Thank the Undying!" said Robin. "The River's saved our lives!"

"They're making up their minds to cross over," said Duck.

They were calling to one another up and down the line. Zwitt kept pointing to our house. We did not realize why until Korib, the miller's son, came past the line with his longbow and knelt to take aim. Korib is a good shot. Hern banged the shutter to just in time. The arrow met it *thock* a fraction after, and burst it open. Hern banged it shut again and heaved the plank across. "Phew!" he said. "Let's go."

"But they'll see us. They'll shoot!" I said. I hardly knew what to do. I nearly wrung my hands like Robin.

"Come along," Hern said. He and Robin took hold of Gull and guided him to the woodshed.

"Just a minute," Duck said. He splashed over to the black pool of the hearth and gathered the Undying down out of their niches. It shocks me even now when I think of Duck picking them up by their heads and bundling them into his arms as if they were dolls.

"No, Duck," said Robin. "Their place is by this hearth. You heard your father say so."

"That," said Duck, "is quite ridiculous nonsense, Robin. The hearth's in the firepots, and the firepots are in the boat. Here." He pushed the Young One into Hern's hands. I noticed Hern did not object. Because Robin was busy with Gull, Duck pushed the One at me. He kept the Lady himself. She has always been his favorite. The One felt heavy in my hands, cold and grainy. I was afraid of him and even more afraid of slipping in the water and losing him. I took him so carefully to the boat that they were all calling out to me to hurry and trying not to call too loud. I could hear Zwitt talking outside. He sounded near. They had a heavy blanket over the boat, hanging over the mast. Robin was holding it down on one side, Duck on the other. Hern had the boat untied and was standing ready to push it out of the shed.

"Get *in*, Tanaqui. You can be religious in the boat," he said. I climbed in carefully and found Gull lying in the bottom where Robin had put him. As soon as I was in, Hern started to push the boat. It was so loaded that he could hardly move it. I pushed up the blanket and offered to help. "Get down!" he snapped, red in the face, with his teeth showing.

As he said it, the boat was through the door, and the current took her sideways along the end of the house, all in seconds. I am not sure whether Hern meant to get in straightaway and did not have time or whether he meant to stay out and push us into deep water. At all events he was still surging through the edge of the floods with his hands on the stern when the boat came out beyond our house, in front of Aunt Zara's, and the Shelling people saw us.

They shouted. I had not seen how they hated us till I heard them shout. It was terrible. Some of them were wading in the water toward our house, and they ran through it toward us. Zwitt slipped over. I hoped he drowned. The others on dry land yelled and pointed at us and cursed. And Korib, on one knee, bent his bow to an arrow again.

"Hern! He's shooting!" I screamed.

Hern was trying to push us sideways into the deep River. He tried to get round to hide behind the boat at the same time. That pushed us the other way. We wove about. Korib shot. It was as good a shot as the first. Hern would be dead, but at that instant we reached the real Riverbank at last, and the ground went from under Hern. He disappeared up to his neck, and the arrow hit the rudder instead. Korib took another and bent his bow again.

Hern had the sense to hang on to the boat. If he had let go then, he would have drowned, for he lost his head completely. "My clothes are heavy!" he screamed. "The River's pulling me down!"

Duck and I climbed about over poor Gull, trying to heave Hern up, and Hern went hand over hand along the boat to keep out of Korib's aim. The boat tipped frighteningly, and Hern's caution was undone, because it spun round and let Korib see him again. The boat was spinning all the time after that. Every time I saw the bank, it was in a different place. Korib kept shooting, at Duck and me as well as at Hern, but we were too busy trying to get Hern aboard to be frightened. Afterward we counted six arrows stuck in the blanket, besides the one in the rudder.

We got Hern up in the end. Robin, by that time, had hooked the tiller in place and was trying to steer, but the boat still went round and round. Hern sat streaming beside Gull, very much ashamed and trying to laugh it off. "When your clothes are full of water, you can't swim, you know," he said. "They weigh a ton." We made him get into dry things.

By this time we were almost at the end of the part of the River we knew, right down to the thick forest.

We had gone that fast. I took the steering from Robin and tried to stop us spinning so. It was not easy. The current ran so strong that if you pushed the boat at all sideways, you were spinning again before you could count five. It took all my skill, but in spite of what my brothers say, I am as good a waterman as they.

"This is dangerous," said Duck, watching me. "We can only go where the River wants. How can we get to the bank?"

Before I could say to Duck what I felt like saying, Gull said suddenly, "We can go where the River wants." He sat up with his back against a thwart. He seemed happy and dreamy, as he used to be when we went fishing on a summer day, and we were sure he was better.

This made us realize—as if we had not known till then—that we had left Shelling far behind, and we were glad. I do not think one of us has ever regretted it. We laughed. We talked over all the lucky things that led to our escape, which is a time none of us will forget, I think, and all the while we were going, fast as a swallow skims, straight down the center of the River, and the trees on the bank seemed to spin about with our speed.

We must have gone leagues that day, and in all those leagues there was nothing on either bank but flooded forest. All there was to see was tall bare trees, with the green just coming to the upper boughs and water winding among their trunks. They had a chilly, slaty look. I confess I was disappointed. It is often the way when you dream of doing something new; it is not so new after all.

When night came on, I tried to work the boat across the current to the eastern bank. Shelling is on the west bank. We did not think Zwitt had sent anyone after us, but we kept to the other side of the River for a number of nights all the same. This caution nearly drowned us that night. The River whirled; the boat whirled and went on whirling, despite all Hern, Robin, and I could do, pulling together at the tiller. Only Gull sat calmly. Duck picked up the Lady and hugged her to his chest. Then the River rushed beneath one side of the boat, and we tipped. I put out my hand and took hold of the One. But he felt so cold and hard that I put him down and picked up the Young One instead. It surprises me still that we came among the trees without sinking. I am sure it was because of our Undying.

We poled and pushed on the trees until we came to higher ground, where we landed and let some of the fire out of our firepots. We cooked pickled trout for supper, and very good it was. Gull seemed so far recovered that he was able to eat for himself.

"I think being back with the River is curing him," Hern said.

That night, after a long quarrel, we decided to sleep in the boat. Hern and Duck were for sleeping on land. Robin, with sound sense, said that if the Shelling men found us, we need only untie the boat to escape. Duck said we could just as easily run away into the forest. In the end Robin said, "Gull's head of the family. Let's ask him. Gull, shall we sleep on the land or in the boat?"

"In the boat," Gull said.

In the middle of the night Gull woke us up shouting and talking. Robin says he talked of disaster and Heathens at first, but when I woke up, he was saying, "All those people! So many people, all rushing. I don't want to go with them. Help!" Then he shouted for my father, and I could hear he was crying.

We all sat up, and Hern got the little lamp lit. Gull seemed to be lying asleep in the boat, but he was talking, and tears were running down his face. Robin bent over him and said, "It's all right, Gull. You're with us. You're safe."

"Where's Uncle Kestrel?" Gull said.

"He brought you to us because that was safest," Robin said.

"I'm not safe from the rushing people," said Gull. "Don't tell me to pull myself together and be a man. They want to take me with them."

We wondered who had told Gull to pull himself together. Probably my father. He was not called the Clam for nothing. He did not like people to talk about their troubles.

"Of course we won't tell you that," said Robin. "We'll keep you safe from everything."

"I want Uncle Kestrel," said Gull. "The people are rushing."

It went on like this for a long time. Each time it seemed that Gull was listening to Robin and she was getting him calmer, he would ask for Uncle Kestrel and talk about these rushing people of his. Robin began to look desperate. Hern and I suggested all sorts of things for her to say to Gull, and she said them, but after another hour it did not seem as if Gull was listening at all.

"What shall we do?" said Robin.

Duck had sat all this while cross-legged and half asleep, hugging the Lady. "Try giving him this," he said, and held out the Lady—by her head, of course.

It worked. Gull put both hands to the Lady and held her to his face. "Thank you," he said. Then he rolled over and went to sleep, with his cheek pressed against the hard wood. I could see Duck looking woeful at losing the Lady, but he did not say anything.

4

From that time on, Gull was worse and worse.

When we woke next morning, we found the floods had risen to cover the place where our fire had been. The tree we had tied the boat to was twenty yards from dry land; after that we always slept in the boat. Gull was awake, too, lying with the print of the Lady on his cheek, but he did not move until Hern started poling us to the higher ground. Then he sat up and called out, "Where are you going? We must get on."

"Why must we get on?" Hern said. He was angry with lack of sleep.

"We must get down to the sea. Quickly," said Gull, and tears ran down his cheeks across the mark of the Lady.

"Of course we will," said Robin. "Be quiet, Hern."

"Why should I? This is the first I've heard about having to get to the sea," Hern said. "What's got into him *now*?"

"I don't know," Robin said helplessly.

This new idea of Gull's gave him no peace, nor us either. Whenever we stopped to eat, he wept and urged us to hurry on to the sea. When we stopped for the night, he was worse still. He kept us all awake talking of Heathens and people rushing and, above all, calling out that we must get on, down to the sea. I grew almost too tired to look at the Riverbanks, which was a pity because the land grew new and interesting after that day. On the day following, the sides of the River were steep hills, covered with a forest, budding all colors from powdery green to bright red, so full of circling birds that they strewed the sky like chaff. Among the trees and birds we saw once a great stone house with a tower like a windmill and a few small windows.

Hern was very interested. He said it looked easy to defend, and if it was empty, it would make a good place for us to live.

"We can't stop here!" Gull cried out.

"It was only an idea, you fool!" Hern said.

Altogether Hern became more and more impatient with Gull. It was hard to blame him, for Gull was very tedious. As the hills held the River in, we floated at a furious pace on a narrow, rushing stream, but we still did not go fast enough for Gull.

"I'd get to the sea tomorrow, if I could, just to shut you up!" Hern said to him.

Duck became as bad as Hern that day. He sighed sarcastically whenever Gull said we must hurry. He and Hern laughed and fooled about instead of helping us look after Gull. I smacked Duck several times, and I would have smacked Hern, too, if I could. I smacked Duck again that night, in spite of Robin shouting at me, when Duck would not let Gull have the Lady.

Duck jumped out on land, hugging the Lady. He was lucky not to fall in the water. We were tied among little brown bushes, with a slope of slimy earth above, where the bank was no bank at all and the River kept slopping our boat into the bushes and away. "She's mine!" Duck shouted, sliding and scrambling above me. "I need her! Give Gull the One. He's strongest."

I was so angry that I tried to climb out after him. But the boat slopped away from the bushes, and Robin caught the back of my rugcoat and hauled me back. "Leave him be, Tanaqui," she said. "Don't you be as bad as he is. Let's try Gull with the One."

We put the dark glistering One in Gull's hand, but he cried out and shuddered. "He's cold. He pulls. Can't we get on now?"

"Some of us have to sleep, Gull," I said. I was nearly as cross as Hern. I gave him the Young One instead, but Gull would not have him either. We had a dreadful night.

In the morning, Duck gave Gull the Lady, looking a little ashamed. But by that time Gull was not having the Lady either. Robin could hardly get him to eat. All he wanted was for us to untie the boat and go on.

"Fun and games all the way to the sea," said Hern. "Then what will he want?"

"I don't think he should go to the sea," said Duck.

"Oh, not you now!" said Hern. "Why not?"

"The Lady doesn't want him to go," said Duck.

"When did she tell you that?" Hern asked jeeringly.

"She didn't," said Duck. "I just had a feeling and knew."

Most of that morning Hern was jeering at Duck for his feeling. Robin snapped at Hern, and I yelled at Duck. We were very tired.

That was the day we came to the lake. The hills on either side of the River seemed to retire away backward, and before we were aware, we were out at one end of a long, winding lake. They tell me it is usually a smaller lake than we saw, but because of the floods, it filled a whole valley. We could see it ahead, white with distance, stretching from mountain to mountain. I think they were real mountains. Their tops went so high that gray clouds sat on them, and they were blue and gray and purple as Uncle Kestrel described mountains. We had never seen such a great stretch of water in our lives as that lake. In the ordinary way we would have been interested. Water in such quantity is restless. It is gray and goes in waves, *chop*, *chop*, *chop*, and lines of foam stretch like ribbons back from the way the waves are going. There was a keen wind blowing.

"What a horrible wind!" Duck said. He crouched down in the boat, hugging his precious Lady.

Hern said disgustedly, "There's *miles* of it! I hate seeing how far I have to go."

Maybe I said that, when I think. Hern and I both found the place too large. As for Gull, he struggled up and stared about. "Why have we stopped?" he said.

We had not stopped, but the current ran weaker in such a mass of water, and I think our boat had turned sideways from it as we came out into the lake. I could see beyond us a wrinkling and a lumping in the lake, more yellow than gray, where the River flood rushed through the larger waters.

"Get the sail up," I said.

"Don't order me about," said Hern. "Get up, Duck, and help."

"Shan't," said Duck. You see how angry we all were.

Hern was stepping the mast when Gull said, "What are you doing? Why can't we get on?"

"I *am* getting on, you mindless idiot!" said Hern. "I'm putting the sail up. Now shut up!"

I do not think Gull listened, but Robin said, "Hern, can't you show poor Gull a bit more sympathy?"

"I *am* sympathetic!" snarled Hern. "But I wouldn't be honest if I pretended I liked him this way. Tell him to keep his mouth shut, if I worry you."

Robin did not answer. We got the mast and the sail up, and Duck condescended to let the keel down. The keel is a thought of my father's, to make a flat riverboat sail well, and it is the best thought he ever had. We raced through the gray waters, leaning. Gull lay quiet in the bottom. Duck sang. When he sings, you know why we call him Duck. Hern told him so. And through their new argument, I noticed Robin still said never a word. She was white and wringing her hands.

"Are you all right?" I said. She annoys me.

"I think we're going to drown," said Robin. "It's so big and so deep! Look at the huge waves!" I would have laughed at her if I had seen the sea then. But the boat did lean, and the water did churn. The shore on both sides was some miles off—too far for swimming—and I thought the lake was deep. I began to be as frightened as Robin. Hern did not say how he felt, but he did not steer near the middle of the lake where the current ran. He kept to one side, and drew nearer to the land there. Shortly we came to a point of land reaching into the lake, with trees on it. The trees grew down to the water's edge and marched on in. We sailed over the tops of trees right under water. Robin's eyes went sideways to them, and she gave a squeak at how deep the lake was. Her hand went out to the One, but she was too much in awe of him to pick him up. She fumbled round till she found the Young One. Her hands went white with clinging to him.

We passed more points of land and more submerged trees and came to a wide bay, where the lake had flooded up a side valley. In the distance we could see a green pasture at the edge of the water. It looked a good place to land. Hern steered that way.

Immediately Gull rose up and screamed at him to

keep straight on. Hern looked at me expressively, and we sailed on.

There was an island on the far side of the bay, a miserable thing where a tuft of willow trees bent over a marsh. Gull let us land there because it was straight ahead. I think it had always been a marshy place, that island, perhaps a saddle of marsh low on the hillside, because around it in a wide ring we saw the heads of rushes—just their heads—pushing above the water. They were tall tanaqui mostly, bravely trying to flower in the Spring. The air was full of their scent as the boat came pushing in among them, disturbing marsh birds every moment.

Hern laughed. "Look! A line of baby brothers!" He pointed to a row of ducklings plodding after their mother among the willows. Duck flounced round with his back to Hern and fell into a deep sulk. Which Hern must have known he would do. My brothers are maddening.

We got out, lit a smoky fire, and ate. Gull would not eat. He just sat with food in his hand. Robin tried thrusting bread in his mouth, but he just sat with it there.

"Oh, I don't know what to do with you, Gull!" Robin cried out. Soon after that she fell asleep, leaning on a willow with the Young One in her lap and Gull sitting sightlessly beside her. Duck was still sulking. Hern and I got up and wandered over the island, but not together. He was at one end, and I was at the other, and I felt I did not care whether I ever saw him again.

I hated that island. The boughs of the willows rattled in the wind, like teeth chattering. They had bright yellow buds on, and the color looked thoroughly dreary against the gray water. The gray water went *crush*, *crush*, *crush*, among the tops of the rushes, bringing their scent in ripples. I looked down at the oily sort of peat under my feet, and I looked out across the gray miles of water to the purple line of land beyond, and I felt truly miserable.

Then I thought I heard my mother's voice behind me. "Tanaqui, for goodness' sake pull yourself together, child!" she said. "Are you too cross to think?"

Naturally I turned round. There was only the empty grove of willows, with Hern's back beyond them, and the other purple shore much nearer but quite as melancholy.

And my mother's voice spoke behind me again, by which I knew I was imagining it, because she would have had to be standing in the water, among the tips of the rushes. "You mustn't let Gull go to the sea, Tanaqui," she said. "Can't you see that? Promise me to stop him."

I turned round again, and of course there was nothing. "Might as well try to stop the River, the way he carries on," I said, just in case she could hear me. Then I thought what a fool I was. I did almost cry, but not quite. I went back to the fire instead.

Gull was not there. I was quite horrified for a moment. Then I found he had got back into the boat and was lying there, staring up at the gray sky. "You'd better stay there," I said to him. I went and looked at Robin, still asleep. I had a feeling, from what Uncle Kestrel said, that my mother had looked a little like Robin. If you look at Robin that way, not just as a person you know very well, she is very pretty. Her face is longish, but round and even, and her eyebrows are quite dark. She always calls her hair yellow and wriggly, but I think that is what people mean when they talk about golden curls. Her eyes are large and blue. Even with her eyes shut, and mauve shadows under them, she was pretty.

She woke up as I looked. "Why are you staring? What's the matter?"

"Gull's gone back to the boat," I said.

"By himself?" said Robin. "Oh, dear, what *is* the matter with him, Tanaqui?"

"He had a bad time in the wars," I said.

Duck came marching across from somewhere, carrying the Lady by her head as usual. "No, it isn't," he said. "Uncle Kestrel told you. The Heathens put spells on him, and now they want him to go to the sea."

"I don't think it's quite like that, Duck, love," Robin said, looking worried. "Tanaqui, I had a dream—"

But I have not heard to this day what Robin's dream was because Hern came rushing back just then, full of brisk talk about getting to the end of the lake by nightfall, and Robin must have forgotten her dream. Whatever it was, it made her happier. She was nothing like so scared of the lake after that.

That lake is huge. We sailed in it all that day and half the next. Beyond the island it became wider yet, until we could barely see the other shore. There were more islands scattered on it, and we learned not to sail too near them, because our keel got tangled with any trees or bushes that grew at their edges before the floods came. We had one lucky escape from a bush and another from a great torn bough, moving on the flood, which I did not see behind the sail.

I think the banks of the lake must have been quite crowded with people before the Heathen came. We saw planks floating and logs cut for winter, hen coops, barrels, and chairs. Duck saw two drowned cats, and I saw a dog. We all saw the corpse except Gull. That was horrible. We came quite near, because Robin insisted the person was alive, until we saw it was only the waves moving her. We thought it was a girl, but she was so small and the clothes so strange that it was hard to be sure. The long hair was browned with the water, but we could see it had been fair and curly.

"It's a Heathen," Duck said. He took the pole and turned her. Her throat was cut. Duck pushed her away with the pole quickly, and then he was sick. We all felt terrible. We none of us said anything, but we knew we did not dare to go near any of our own people. That corpse looked just like us.

We met no one living all the length of that lake. Once or twice we thought we saw other corpses, but we did not go near them. Nobody was sailing except us. Later in the day it rained. A big purple cloud hung over us, lower than the rest of the sky, and rain soused down on us out of it. Behind us the lake was silver with sun, and in front of us a mighty rainbow came down across some dark green pine trees growing on a point of land and buried itself in the lake at their roots. We saw the trees sunlit through the colors of the rainbow. But the rain cloud hung above us. "Just like our bad luck does," Duck said gloomily.

That point of land was a long way off. By the time we reached it, night was coming on and we decided to tie up there. Gull protested, but we were getting used to that.

"I'm sorry, Gull," Robin said. "We have to stop for the night." From Robin, that is steely firmness.

Gull would not get out of the boat. We all pulled and pushed at him, but he would not move. In the end we had to pole the boat round the point, where it was sheltered from the wind, and pull it up out of the water with Gull still in it. We did that because we did not trust him not to sail away while we were getting supper. In that place the land fell back and a marshy stream came down to meet the lake. The lake had come up to meet the stream a long way. Nowhere was dry. Rushes of all sorts grew there, and the flag irises were green already, with brown water round their roots. The evening filled with the scent of tall tanaqui and the smell of damp smoke. Robin could not get the fire to go.

"Look," said Duck, pointing down to where the reeds grew away under the water. A heron was standing there, with its head bent, looking for fish. "Look, a big brother, with long legs like sticks." Trust Duck to remember Hern's insult.

Hern roared with rage and dived at Duck.

Duck fled down among the tall rushes, hugging the Lady. "And a long nose!" he screamed back. Hern went galloping and squelching and roaring after him.

"Oh, go and stop them, Tanaqui!" Robin said. She was crouching over the fire, blowing it.

I went down among the rushes after my brothers, grumbling. I think it was too bad of them still. I could see where Hern had gone, from the path of trodden rushes and deep footprints filling with oily water, but even though it was getting dark, I was fairly sure that Duck had doubled back and was lying low uphill somewhere. When I came to the lake, all the light was in the water, and Hern was an angry shadow against it, with his head bent, glaring for Duck along the sopping shore. We were facing the pine trees on the point there, looking across the bay of muddy water from the stream and the lake.

Hern looked so like a heron, standing there, that I nearly laughed as I said, "Duck didn't come this way."

Hern turned round, saw I was laughing, and raised his hand to hit me. I turned to run away.

Then we neither of us moved because our mother's voice said, "Hern! Tanaqui!"

We both turned the same way, to look out across

the gloomy inlet. From that I know Hern heard it as well as I did. And I know I saw a shape standing there, in the mist above the water, whatever Hern says. I saw the dark body with a blur of whiter hair and a smudge of white face. The same voice said, "Stop fighting and look after Gull. You mustn't let him go to the sea, whatever you do. Take him down to the watersmeet."

"Take him where?" I said. "Mother, what's wrong with Gull?" I heard Hern laughing while I said it. "What's so funny?" I said.

"You standing there talking to trees and stones and half the boat," Hern said. "Take a look."

As he spoke, I saw it was true. The stern of the boat came out of the reeds a short way, with water showing beneath, and that was the lower half of the dark shape. The upper half was the trunk of a pine tree that seemed exactly above it. And above that I saw dimly that a bush was budding around a light-colored rock, high up on the point, making the hair and the face. "But there was a voice," I said. "You heard the voice."

"The heron," said Hern. There was indeed a bird crying out. The cries grew fainter as I listened, and I heard wingbeats. "We're all tired out," said Hern. "That's what did it. I just hope Gull lets us get a proper night's sleep tonight, or we'll be as bad as he is."

"It didn't seem like being tired," I said. I felt very foolish.

"Well, it wasn't Mother," said Hern. "She's dead. I admit I made the same mistake for a second, but don't say a word to Robin, will you? You'll only upset her."

I agreed to that. So many things upset Robin. We went back among the rushes and helped Robin get supper. Duck appeared when it was ready. Hern gave him a look in the firelight, but he did not say anything, and Duck sat down hugging the Lady and said nothing either.

Gull would not eat. He lay in the boat, growing colder and colder, and would only say, "Why can't we go on?" Robin heaped all our blankets around him, but he never grew warm. Nor would he eat in the morning. But at least he was quiet that night. Duck gave him the Lady without being asked, and we had hours of good sleep.

We went on down the lake next day. By the middle of the morning we could see the high purple land standing right across our way, and we thought it was the end of the lake. But we could see no way for the River to flow out. Hern said that it must flow out, since the current in the middle of the lake was still strong. We agreed that we would eat lunch somewhere on the high purple shore and then look for the rest of the River. So as the land approached, Hern took down the sail, intending to row to the rocks on the shore. For all our knowledge of the River, we were fooled into doing that. The lake looked smooth and calm, and the rocks ahead were so vast that we did not see how fast we were moving until the sail was down. Then we saw we were not stopping. The crates and barrels and driftwood went with us at the same speed as before, and the mountain strode toward us.

"Oh good!" said Gull, lying in the bottom of the boat. "We're really getting on."

"I shall hit him!" said Hern, with his mouth pulled like a grin. "I shall really hit him!" He lugged the oars aboard again, because they did nothing but turn us this way and that, and fell on the sail, trying to hoist it again.

"Don't do that!" Robin and I shrieked. The wind had gone, because we were right under the mountain, and the boat tipped horribly. Hern looked up to argue, but by then we were speeding straight at a huge cliff, and he put his arm over his head instead.

It looked as if we were going to crash into that cliff. You think a great many things very quickly when you see death coming. I thought: It's a bad thing, the way Gull wants to get on! Bad, bad! and at the same time I wondered why there were no great waves dashing on the rock ahead. The water was all smooth, stretched smooth and rapid, with only a few yellow bubbles at the edge.

And then *jerk*. I thought my head had come off my neck. The boat turned in a wrench as the current turned, and we were thrown past the cliff into a narrow gap of roaring water.

Here the rushing was as loud as the night the floods came, with echo upon echo shouting within that. The big walls of rock were so high on either side that there seemed almost no light, and the sky a ribbon high above. The look I snatched at it showed great trees growing in the sides of the rock, looking small as bushes. But I could not keep my eyes off the River. I could not have done as Hern did and taken the keel up. I hung on to the sides of the boat and stared at the foaming water. It was crushed and tormented into a small space with great rocks in it, which tattered it into riding waves, threw it in spouts, and spun it in glassy circles. Our boat spun and tossed and raced with it. One moment we were in the center, white under the light, and the next we were in black water at the sides of the gorge. Far down below in the black water, I could see ferns and grass growing, deep down on the sides of the cliff. I tried to shut my eyes—it was so deep—and went on staring in spite of myself.

I thought I heard screaming voices. I paid no attention until something came battering into the water just by the bows of the boat. The boat slewed round. I saw the spout of a splash just falling back into the water and looked up. There were tiny people up there, on top of the cliffs, black against the sky, and a thin bridge stretched across the gap. It had been broken. Two thicker halves stuck out on either side, and the center had been mended with planks. I saw the light between the planks. The bridge was lined with round heads, and beside each head was a ragged round lump of rock, ready to drop on us.

"They think we're Heathens!" Robin screamed. She dragged a blanket over her head and Duck's, and half over Gull, too. Hern and I were left outside. There was nothing we could do. Our boat swirled toward the bridge. The rocks moved, hung, and then got larger and larger, and we found our heads jerking up to watch and then down at the furious River, not knowing what to look at. All round us were spouts of water as the rocks came down. They jerked us this way and that, and I think it was the jerking that saved us. We were splashed all over, but nothing hit us. Then, before we had time to feel glad, there was more light and Hern was screaming there were rapids ahead.

We were through the falls the same moment. There was a lurch and a swoop, and the boat's nose went down, heaving more water over Hern and me. After that we were out and sliding a boiling, racing width of water most of the way across a second smaller lake. I think the falls were not steep, but I did not dare look back. Sometimes I wake up at night thinking I hear the chunking splash of rocks coming down in the River, and I still tremble all over.

‖ 5 ‖

THIS IS TO BE a very big rugcoat. We have been here in the old mill for days and days now, and though I am weaving close and fine, I have still not half finished my story. Even so, I think I shall finish it long before Robin is well. She is more fretful every day, and her face is the color of candles. I find it so hard to be patient with her. That is why I am weaving. When Uncle Kestrel first brought me my loom and my wheel and my wool, I was sick with impatience, and it all went so slowly. I had to spin my wool and set up the threads on the loom, and even when I began to weave, it took half the morning on the first sentence. But now I have found how to go fast. I set the first part of the pattern and cast the threads, there and back, and then the row to hold it, and while I do that, I am thinking of my next line. By the time I have finished that band of words, I often have the next three or four ready in my head. I go faster and faster, click and clack, change the threads with my feet, click and clack with the shuttles, and so on. And the story grows in the loom.

We swept out of that second lake into the wide, muddy River again. I found I was holding the One in both hands. I never remember picking him up, but my hands were cold and numb with holding him. Robin, with her face very white, was just laying down the Young One. Duck, of course, had the Lady.

"You might have let Gull have her!" I said.

"He doesn't need her," Duck said sulkily. Gull did look peaceful. His eyes were closed, as if nothing had happened. "And I did need her," Duck said. "She went all warm and I knew we'd be safe."

"Of course she's warm, the way you hug her all the time!" I said. "It's a wonder she's not worn down to a log."

"Shut up, Tanaqui," Robin said wearily. "Let's find somewhere to have lunch."

We did not find anywhere to land. The River had spread between hills that must have been nearly a mile apart. There were the roofs of barns and houses sticking up out of the swirling water on both sides of us. We had some thoughts of tying up to the first roofs we came to, but when we reached them, two old people stood up by the chimneys and yelled insults at us. They thought we were Heathens. We put the sail up and went on, eating cold food as we sailed, feeling very dejected. Gull would not eat again. "I'm glad we're getting on," he kept saying.

We did not get on very well. The River turned, and the wind blew from the north, in gusts, straight in our faces. We had to tack from side to side against it. Often we found we were sailing right round a submerged roof, and nearly every one was burned or broken. We smelled burning the whole way. Up on the hills to either side were the burned ruins of more houses, burned haystacks, and burned woods. Where the trees were alive, they were not budding. It was like sailing back into winter. Just a few of the fields had been plowed in spite of the wars, and the earth was a curious red, as if the ground was wounded.

"The Heathens have been here," Hern said. "Everyone's run away."

None of us answered him. I think we were all becoming more and more uneasy at the way Gull insisted on our going toward where the Heathens must be. I know I was. It seemed to me we were in danger from both sides, and I began to wonder at how thoughtlessly we had set off into this danger. True, Zwitt had left us no choice, but there was no reason to have gone down the River more than a mile or two. I wondered why we were going on, and I wished my father were there to tell us what to do.

Toward evening the River rushed again between steep hills of reddish earth that were covered in bare trees. Someone among the trees shot arrows at us. They all fell short as we raced with the flood, but after that we kept a blanket over us, and whichever of us was steering wrapped their head in a rugcoat. We did not dare think of landing until the River widened again and rushed past on either side of islands, long and boat-shaped and half submerged. The first islands were crowded with people who must have fled there from the Heathens. They were dark-haired, like Shelling people. As soon as they saw the boat, they crowded to the edge of the floods, shouting, "You can't land here! No room!" Zwitt could hardly have been friendlier.

Duck was steering. He stood up and put his tongue out at them, the fool, and the rugcoat slipped off his head. Then they all screamed, "Heathen!" and threw sticks and stones after us. We kept clear of all the other islands until night came on.

As it grew dark, we could see fires here and there on the steep shores and the islands. But the last island we came to was dark. It was very small, with only one patch of dry ground under the trees. Robin said we must land there. She was tired out. We were all scared of landing. We drew in as quietly as we dared and went ashore whispering, even though there was no one there. We lit our fire in a hole among the roots of a tree and prayed to our Undying that nobody would see it.

Gull would not eat again. He would not speak, and he was cold. But we were all cold that night. We pressed against one another in the boat, and every time I woke, the rest of them were shivering, too. I was woken by a dream I kept having. As far as I remember, it was just my mother's voice, saying, "The watersmeet!" and with it a slight scent of tanaqui. But I find it hard to separate it in my head from the dream I have been having ever since I started weaving. In that dream I see my mother bending over me, just the shape of her, with fair hair as curly as Robin's, but bushy like mine. "Wake up, Tanaqui," she is saying. "Wake up and think!" There is a scent of tanaqui with that dream, too. And I do think I have been thinking, but nothing comes of it, except that I blame myself.

In the morning the boat, our blankets, the ground, and the bare trees were all covered with frost. It looked odd, the white frost on the bloodred earth. The River here ran pink among the yellow, because of the earth.

Gull would not eat again, and I thought of my dream. I found I was wringing my hands like Robin as I looked down at Gull lying in the frosty boat. I expect it was the cold. Now what is a watersmeet? I said to myself. It is where one river joins another. Hern may say what he likes, but if we do come to another river, I shall fall overboard, or pretend to die, or something, and make sure we stay there.

Then it turned out that Robin had come to a decision, too. "You know," she said, "I don't think we should go any farther. I think we should stay on this island and get Gull warm and well again. I think this is the safest place we're going to find."

Gull, for a wonder, said nothing. He seemed too

weak to speak. But Duck said, "Oh, honestly, Robin! We'd starve here!"

Hern said, "We'd be much better off finding a deserted house somewhere. Gull needs shelter, Robin."

"Or there must be *some* people who'll believe we're not Heathens," I said, "and who'll help us look after him. Let's go on, please."

"I think you're wrong," Robin said. "It seems to me we may be killing Gull, taking him on a journey like this."

"He wanted to go," Hern said.

"He doesn't know what's right for him," Robin said. "Do let's stay."

We took no notice. Hern and Duck climbed over Gull in the boat and put the sail up. I poured water on the fire and put the firepot away.

Robin sighed and shook her head and looked about eighty. "Oh, I don't know what to do for the best!" she said. "Promise me you'll stop as soon as you see a good place."

We all promised, easily and dishonestly. I meant only to stop at another river. I do not know what Hern and Duck meant to do, but I can tell when they are being dishonest.

As we sailed on, the sun came up over the hill at the right of the River, leaving it all dark and blue with frost and turning the left bank to gold. The slopes became higher and steeper as we swirled along, one blue, one gold, until the sun melted the red earth into sight again. There were low red cliffs to the left suddenly, which stopped like the wall of a red house. Beyond that the River was twice as wide or more than that. We could see a row of trees to either side, standing in water, and sheets of water beyond that, flaring in the sun. I think the trees marked the real low banks of the wide River.

I turned my head as we sailed past the end of the red cliff. And I saw more water there, winding back behind the cliffs, with red cliffs on the other side of it.

"The watersmeet!" I shouted. I jumped to the tiller and wrestled to get it out of Hern's hand. Duck jumped with me.

"Don't be idiots!" Hern shouted.

We went to and fro and the sail swung. The boat began going in circles. "What are you doing?" Robin shouted.

"We're going to land. We want to land!" Duck yelled.

With three of us shouting and fighting round the tiller and the boat going in circles, we should have been a perfect mark for bowmen, Heathen or our own. But we were lucky. Hern gave in, though he kept shouting. We came surging round into a great bed of rushes under the first red cliff.

They were the tallest rushes I have ever seen. They must have been deep in the floods beneath, but they were high above our heads even so. They parted in front of the boat and closed behind, and the speed we had drove us on between them, still arguing, into a sort of green grove, until we grounded on a beach of dry shingle, hidden from both rivers.

"I suppose this seems safe enough," Robin was saying when a Heathen man came swiftly down a small red path above us and stopped among the rushes when he saw us.

"Who was it called?" he said.

He seemed—how shall I say?—wet with haste or damp with the open air. His skin was ruddier than ours. Otherwise he was not so different, except that he was grown up and four of us were not. His hair was long and golden and even more wildly curly than Robin's or Duck's. I must say I liked his face. He had a gentle, laughing look, and his nose turned up a little. His rugcoat was an old faded red one, not unlike the one my father went to war in, very plain and wet with dew. I could see there was red mud splashed on his legs and that he wore shoes like ours, wet, too. But to our relief, he had no kind of weapon. His hands were empty, spread to part the rushes.

I thought: Well, if this is a Heathen, they can't be so very bad.

"Er—nobody called, really," Hern said, cautiously. "We were arguing about whether to land or not."

"It's lucky you did land," he said. "There's a large party of Heathens in a boat coming down the Red River." Since they were Heathens to him, we knew he meant our people. Not that this made any difference in the danger to us.

We looked at one another. "We'd better wait until they're past," Robin said doubtfully.

"If you like, you can come up to my shelter to wait," the Heathen man said politely.

We did not like this idea, but we did not want him to know we were his enemies. Robin and Hern and I looked at one another again. Duck looked at the Heathen man and smiled. "Yes, please," he said. I kicked at his ankle, but he just moved out of the way. The next second he was scampering away up the path. Robin gave a small ladylike wail and climbed out of the boat, too.

Hern and I did not know what to do. We thought we ought to stay together, but that meant leaving Gull. We bent down and tried to pull Gull up.

"Come along, Gull," I said. "We're going on a visit." Hern said encouraging things, too, but Gull would not move, and we could not budge him.

Damp hair brushed my face, and I jumped. The Heathen man was kneeling beside the boat and leaning between us to look at Gull. "How long has he been like this?" he said.

Hern looked at me. "Months, I think."

Robin leaned eagerly over us. "Do you know what's wrong with him, sir? Can you help us?"

"There's something I can do," the Heathen man said. "I wish you could have brought him here before this, though." He stood up, looking very serious. "We must wait till the Heathen have gone by," he said.

Duck came scooting back down the path. "I saw the Heathen—" he said.

"Quiet!" said the man.

We heard loud voices and the splashy sound of many people rowing. I never saw the people, and they were all talking at once, but I heard one say, "All clear ahead. None of the devils about." It sounded like a big, heavy boat, moving fast with oars and current, and I thought they must be patrolling for Heathen. The sounds moved quickly into the wide stretch of the double River and faded away.

When they had gone, our Heathen said, "My name is Tanamil, which means Younger Brother."

I was not sure we should tell him our names, for fear he might guess we were not Heathens, not having outlandish names like his. But Robin went all polite and ladylike and introduced us all. "This is Hern," she said, "and Tanaqui, and my brother lying there is Gull. That is Duck—"

Tanamil looked up at Duck, in the path above. "Duck?" he said. "Not Mallard?"

Duck's face went almost as red as the earth. "Mallard," he said. "Duck's a baby name."

Tanamil nodded and looked back at Robin. "I can guess your name," he said. "You have to be a bird, too, a bright one, a bird of omen. Robin?"

Robin went red, too, and nodded. She was so confused she forgot to be ladylike. "How did you guess?"

Tanamil laughed. He had a very pleasant laugh, that

I admit, very joyful. It made us want to laugh, too. "I've wandered about collecting knowledge," he said. Then he went serious as he looked down at Gull. "And lucky I did," he said. "He's very far gone."

We all looked at Gull then, thinking Tanamil was exaggerating—until we saw how Gull had changed, even in that short time. He was thinner and paler than ever. He lay with his eyes closed, breathing so slightly that we could hardly see it. We could see the other bones in his head, joining those sharp cheekbones of his. He looked like a skull.

Robin seized Tanamil's arm. She would never have done such a thing in the ordinary way. It shows how upset she was. "What *is* the matter with him? Do you know?"

Tanamil continued to look down at Gull. "Yes," he said. "I know. They are trying to take his soul. He has fought them long and hard for it, but they are winning."

Hern gave a sort of shiver. He was angry. He is always angry when people talk this way, but I had never seen him as angry as he was then. "Oh, are they?" he said. "And who are *they* in that case, and where are you imagining they are?" He was so angry he could hardly speak.

Tanamil was not offended. He seemed to understand Hern. "The one who is reeling your brother in now," he said, "is a powerful man who sits beyond the edge of my knowledge. I think he is down by the sea."

Hern seemed not to know what to say next. He did not seem angry anymore. "Gull kept saying he must go to the sea," I said.

"Then the man who wants him is there," Tanamil said. "Now I must get to work. We must save your brother without this powerful man suspecting. You understand?" He looked at us all very solemnly. "If what I do seems strange to you, it is done for the best. Will you remember that?"

"Yes," we all said, nodding, even Hern, though I had expected him to object. For all Tanamil was a Heathen, we felt we trusted him. He seemed to know so much.

He told us to get out of the boat and stand beside him in the rushes. We all did so willingly, leaving Gull lying in the bottom of the boat. Tanamil squatted down by the water's edge, where he dug and prized in the ground with his fingers until he had a double handful of wet red earth. We watched, mystified, as he dumped his pile of earth on the dry part of the path and set to work, squeezing, pinching, molding, smoothing at it. Occasionally he glanced in the boat to see how Gull was doing, and continued molding the earth. Shortly Hern began to look sarcastic. The earth was becoming a man-shaped figure, a young man-shaped figure, a figure we could recognize.

"It's Gull!" Duck whispered. "Isn't it *like* him!"

It is very like him. I have it in front of me as I weave. It is Gull to the life, but not so thin as he was when he lay in the boat. The wonder of it is that

Tanamil caught the Gull he could not have known—the Gull who once laughed and boasted about going to war, and poled about the River whistling because he found life good. I can remember Gull like that—and an awful tease—but how could Tanamil have known?

When the figure was finished, Tanamil sat comfortably down in the rushes and said, "You can sit down if you want." Only Hern did so. The rest of us stood watching anxiously. Tanamil brought out from his rugcoat a slender reddish pipe, which seemed to be made of a bundle of thin reeds, and began to play it. After the first few notes Hern, who had been scornfully plaiting rushes, looked up, fascinated. It was a sad, sobbing tune that seemed to have a thread of laughter running through it. The notes ran, caught themselves, blended, and ran on, singing. I saw Duck's mouth open and Robin's face entranced. That pipe chimed like bells and ran like water. In it I felt all Spring budding and bursting as it does along the Riverside, and yet it was Spring in the future, overlaid by a sad winter. I hoped it would never stop. I wanted it to run forever as the River does.

I looked down at the red figure of Gull standing in the path. It was drying. I could see it turning pinker, shrinking a little, flaking slightly, and plainly becoming harder every second. I could have sworn the notes of the pipe were sucking water from it and then baking it under my eyes. It became harder, pinker, and smaller yet, until it seemed impossible that any moisture was left in it. Tanamil still played, watching the image as he played, until the pink was whitish. Then he drew to a close so gently that I did not at first realize he had stopped. There was no silence. There was the sound of the two rivers running on either side of us, and the wind stirring the reeds, and birds on the cliffs. All these noises seemed to have caught and held the music.

"*OH!*" said Robin, like a scream. "Gull—!"

I looked into the boat and Gull was transparent. I could see the boards and a corner of the blanket beneath him. I could see how the hair at the back of his head was pressed flat as he lay. As I looked, he was fainter. He was like a pool of liquid with his own reflection in it, and the liquid seemed to be drying up. It shrank, still with the whole of Gull in it, and dwindled till it lay only in the space in front of the tiller.

Hern jumped up. His foot went out to kick the dry image.

"Don't touch it!" Tanamil said, quick as a bark.

Hern's foot went back to the ground. At the same instant the liquid Gull dried away entirely. There was nothing but an empty boat.

We stood staring, with pale faces, too shocked to speak. Tanamil put his pipe away, stood up, and gently moved the image of Gull from the red earth. "There," he said, with Gull in his hands. "He's safe now."

"Safe how?" said Robin.

"Where is he?" said Duck.

"What have you done?" I said. As for Hern, he was speechless.

Tanamil held the dry pink Gull out to Robin, and she took it, utterly dismayed. "What—what do I do with *this*?" she said.

"Keep him safe until you come to your grandfather," Tanamil said.

"We haven't got a grandfather," said Duck.

Tanamil looked round at us all as if he did not know what to say. "I didn't know how little you understood," he said at last. He considered a moment; then he said, "Gull's soul is not usual. If an enemy took it, he could use it as a spout to drain off the souls of his soul, as it were, and draw through it the souls of his forebears, right down to his first ancestor. I do not know if the man who was trying to take it knows this, but I know he should not have a chance to find out. What I have done makes Gull's soul safe without this man being any the wiser. If I swear by your Undying that Gull is safe, will you believe me?"

"He's safe from us, too, by the look of it," Robin said, and Tanamil laughed.

"Come up to my shelter and warm yourselves," he said, "before you go on."

I do not know how we came to agree to this. Tanamil was a Heathen. He had just taken Gull from us, and the way he had done it proved him to be a powerful magician. Yet we thought of none of these things. We went up the red path between the rushes with him, Robin carrying Gull.

The path came up on a grassy shoulder beneath the red cliff. From there we could see into both rivers.

Our own River wound back in a high gorge, mighty, swift, and yellow. The other River ran red and was smaller, though no less swift, and it had a merriment about it that I had not seen in a River before. It sang between red walls. The trees, ferns, and reeds seemed greener there. It was full of birds. We heard the noise of birds at all times while we were with Tanamil.

When I remember Tanamil's shelter, I am confused. I thought it was built against the face of the red cliff, of red mud and driftwood, and that we pushed reeds aside to go in. But I could swear that we went inside the cliff itself. Indeed, we must have been inside the cliff, for I remember a second entrance low down beside the second River, where the red water slapped robustly among the fringed tops of tanaqui. The sunlight came in green through it and danced on the ceiling in curls and ripples.

Inside was a comfortable room enough, with chairs, a table and piles of rugs, some of fur, some woven plain, and a good fire blazing. Tanamil had no Undying at his hearth, Heathen that he was. Robin carefully put the dry little image of Gull there instead. Seeing her do that broke the spell that was on me for an instant—I am now sure that it was a spell. I jumped up, saying, "Oh! We left our Undying in the boat!"

Tanamil smiled his pleasant smile at me. "Don't worry. They'll guard the boat for you."

I sat down again, and for a long time I did not remember we were on a journey or consider our danger or even think of Gull. I had the time of my life instead.

We all did, although Robin did not seem to enjoy herself so much at the end. But I cannot remember much that happened. Up till now it was all confused in my head. But by thinking and thinking and discussing it with Duck, I have remembered it better—though I am not sure we have it in the right order.

"That's the trouble with you, Tanaqui," Duck said to me. "You always have to have things in *order*. You're as bad as Hern."

I think Duck is right, though I did not realize it before. If I cannot get a thing straight in my head, it offends me, like a piece of weaving that has gone wrong—like Robin's awful blue skirt. This is why Hern and I are so much more horrified than Duck by our strange time with Tanamil.

:❙ 6 ❙:

I REMEMBER WE HAD an excellent meal by that good fire. It was food such as I had only heard of before, lobster and fine white cakes and venison, with dried grapes afterward. Uncle Kestrel told us of grapes. They grow among the trees of the Black Mountains, on trailing creepers. When I first heard of the King, my father said he ate lobster and venison every day. I never thought to have them myself. We had wine, too, like our King. Wine is fine pink stuff with a sparkle to it. Tanamil said it was from the Black Mountains. Robin poured a little of hers in front of the dry statue of Gull. Tanamil laughed at her for doing it, and Robin went very pink. But Duck says she did it again at supper.

Now the odd thing is that I remember only that one

meal. We must have had another, because we stayed the night. Indeed, I remember sitting out beneath the cliff in the hot sun, looking at both rivers and eating, not once but several times. Yet when I think, I only remember that one meal in front of the fire.

Hern and Duck got very merry. They romped and rolled and fought in the heaps of rugs. I think I did, too, but not all the time. I watched Robin dancing. Robin often used to dance in Shelling when she had time, but she never danced as she did then, when Tanamil played his pipe for her. I remember her dancing in the room, with whorls and wrinkles of sunlight sliding on the ceiling above her, and outside on the grass. I even seem to remember her up on the cliff opposite, across the second River, but that must be nonsense. What I do remember is that she took hold of Tanamil's arm on several occasions, demanding that he pipe for her. That is quite unlike Robin. She is so shy and formal. But I know she did. And when she asked him, Tanamil smiled and piped for her again, clear and lovely music, like a dream of music. And Robin danced and danced.

Duck wanted to learn to pipe, too. Hern and I made an outcry at that. If you ever heard Duck sing! But Tanamil obligingly went out and cut hollow reeds for him. I remember his fingers flying as he cut holes in the reeds and bound them together. He made the mouthpieces from joints in the reeds, where the pith is solid. Then he put Duck's fingers to the holes and told him to blow. Duck blew. Nothing happened.

"Silence! Thank goodness!" said Hern.

"Try saying *Ptehwh*! to it," said Tanamil.

"*Ptehwh!*" said Duck, scarlet in the face. And all the pipes sounded a terrible squealing and braying, as if pigs had got among donkeys. We shrieked with laughter. Duck glowered at us and went outside through the second door, down beside the red River. Shortly we heard halting little tunes from among the rushes.

Hern raised his eyebrows at me. "Ye gods! I didn't think he knew any tunes."

Tanamil taught Hern things, too. I remember them squatting together in the dust, and Tanamil drawing things there with a pointed stick, and Hern nodding. At other times they were leaping on one another and wrestling. I liked the look of that. I pulled Tanamil's arm, like Robin, and said, "Show me, too!"

He showed me. There were things I could not do, not being as strong as Hern, but he showed me the way to use a person's own strength against him. I think that if a grown enemy—say, Zwitt—walked into this mill at the moment, I could throw him to the ground and maybe kill him. But I am not sure that I should use this knowledge. I think of who it was taught me.

Two things Tanamil taught me I *have* used. I forget how it came about, but I know I told him that there were many words I did not know how to weave. He said there was no harm in making your own patterns, provided you taught others what you meant. But he said, "You must use the right pattern for River. That is important," and he showed me, weaving with rushes. He also showed me a more expressive way of twisting yarn. He had me twist rushes until I could do it. He said, "When you use yarn twisted this way, use it for the strongest parts of your story. Your meaning will leap from the cloth." I have done this in several places. I do not mind that it was Tanamil who taught me. It works.

I asked Hern what Tanamil was showing him in the dust with the pointed stick, but he would not tell me.

Later on I remember Tanamil coming to us when the firelight was leaping on the ceiling and mixing with the ripples of sun there. "There's a question you must all ask me," he said. "Each of you ask."

None of us could think what to say. I was reminded of the way Aunt Zara *will* say, "Tanaqui, there is a little word you should say to me. What is it?" And of course I can never think what she means, so I do not say it, and she calls me rude. If only she would say, "Tanaqui, you haven't said please," then I should know what she meant and say it. It was like that with Tanamil. He wanted us to say something particular, which was obvious to him, but not at all to us.

Hern said first, "Would you call yourself a magician?"

"In some ways, yes," said Tanamil, "but that is not what I call myself." And he turned to Duck.

"Do you believe in the Undying?" Duck asked. He had been thinking earnestly, and I could see he thought he was very clever asking this.

Tanamil was amused. He turned his face to the

flickering roof and laughed. "Not as you do," he said. "But they exist." Then he turned to me, still laughing.

For a moment I thought I knew what he wanted me to ask, and then it was gone.

"No, no," he said. "You must ask what you *want* to ask."

This was like Aunt Zara saying I must say please because I wanted to—and who does? "Please," I said, but that was not it, of course. "Where do you come from?" I said.

It was not the right question. He laughed again. "I suppose you would say I come from the Black Mountains."

I puzzle over this more and more, because I know the Heathens come from the sea. While I puzzled then, Tanamil turned to Robin. And I do not know what Robin asked. I know she asked, and I think she asked right, and that Tanamil answered, but I have no memory of what was said. Duck says I do not remember because Robin was not there at the time. He says Tanamil came and asked each of us separately, and he says I do wrong to put it in here because it happened right at the beginning of our stay. But I remember it almost at the end, and I am weaving this story.

The next things happened in the night, and I know that was right at the end. We were all asleep among the rugs by the fire. It was more comfortable and warm than we had been since we left home, so I do not know why I woke up, unless it was that Robin and Tanamil were making such a noise with their argument. I only heard a few things they said. I kept falling asleep and waking again to hear them still heatedly at it. I will put what I heard.

Tanamil was saying, "But they're bound to go. They all bound themselves, and I can't keep them forever."

"In that case," Robin said, "I shall have to go, too."

"But you never bound yourself," Tanamil said. "Why should you go?"

Robin said, "I did. I promised my mother, years ago—"

"If your mother knew what I was asking," Tanamil said quickly, "she would tell you to do as I say." That struck me as unfair. Tanamil did not know what my mother would say. But Robin is always saying and thinking that our mother would want this and not like that, and I am sure Tanamil knew it. Robin began to cry. "All I'm asking is that you stay here with me," he said.

All he was asking! I did not care to have Robin bullied like this. I meant to sit up and tell Tanamil a thing or two, but I went to sleep instead.

I woke up to hear Robin shouting, "I tell you *no!*"

And Tanamil shouted back, "*Why?* Why, why, *why?*"

"Because of what you are," Robin said. She was crying again—or still. "It wouldn't be right." I could have shaken her. She had as good as told him we were not Heathens.

"How do you mean, not right?" Tanamil demanded. "Where's the difference between us?"

"Age, for a start," said Robin.

"What a feeble thing to say!" said Tanamil. He sounded as disgusted as Hern would have been. But I was glad because I could see Robin was trying to cover up her mistake. "Have you any other silly excuses?" he said.

"They're not excuses; they're reasons," Robin said coldly.

"That was unfair. I apologize," said Tanamil.

I thought that in spite of her mistakes, Robin was dealing with him better than I could have done. I must have gone to sleep thinking it. When I woke up next, Robin was getting the worst of it.

"I can't see how you can know that!" she was bleating, in her feeblest way.

"I do," said Tanamil. "Next to Gull, you're the one most at risk. I'm not just saying it to persuade you—"

"Then why are you saying it?" said Robin.

"A hit," Tanamil said. "Robin, I can't see much of the future, but I don't like what I see. Stay here and let the others go. They've inherited his toughness. You haven't."

This gave Robin the moral advantage. She is good at taking that. "And what would you think of me if I drew back just because I was born feeble?" she asked.

That must have been the winning answer. When I woke up again, Tanamil was not in the room and Robin was asleep just beside me. This time it was Duck who had woken me. He was crouched beside me, half rosy in the fire, and the other half of him caught in whorls and ripples of moonlight from the River beyond the door.

"Tanaqui," he whispered, "I've just remembered something. You know that boatload of people Tanamil said were Heathens?"

"Yes," I said. I was suddenly full of distrust for Tanamil. He had taken Gull, and now he was trying to take Robin. I wondered how we had been mad enough to stay with him. I knew he must have cast a spell to make us, and I was scared silly. "What about them?" I said. "They weren't Heathens, they were our people, weren't they?"

"No," whispered Duck. "That was the funny thing. They were real Heathens. They had hair a bit like ours and brown faces—like his—and peculiar clothes with iron hats. Why did *he* call them Heathens?"

Hern was sitting up on the other side of the fire. "Are you sure?" he whispered.

"Positive. I *saw* them," said Duck.

We all looked at the small pale figure of Gull sitting on the hearth. I felt sick. Hern said, "Then he knew who we were from the start. We—"

There was a rilling, splashing noise outside. The rushes at the entrance bobbed, and the moonlight was drowned in the shadow of Tanamil, wading in the water. We dived into our rugs and lay there, so that he would not know we were awake. And we all went to sleep. Duck and Hern remember nothing beyond diving into the blankets either.

Next morning Tanamil was gone. The shelter was

as I remembered it when I first started to think about it, built of old wood and red earth, leaning against the cliff. The one door was open to the sun on the grassy shoulder between the two rivers. It was cold. The fire was out, and I think there were no longer any blankets. There were certainly none when I looked back into the shelter before we left. We got up and hurried into the sun, shivering.

Robin was there first, holding the little figure of Gull. "I take it he means us to go," she said dourly. "I think he might have said good-bye."

"He might have given us breakfast," said Duck.

"We've got food in the boat," said Hern. "Come on."

The boat was there, bobbing in a green cave among the reeds, with our food and the Undying still in her.

"I'm relieved to see that," said Hern. "Get in. Let's eat as we go."

"Why the hurry?" I said.

"Who's bossy?" said Duck.

"*I'm head of the family!*" Hern shrieked, turning on him. "Do as I say!"

Duck and I both turned to Robin. She looked at the clay image between her hands and shrugged. "I suppose that's the truth of it," she said.

"Then he'd better be polite about it," Duck said. We glowered at Hern, Duck and I.

"I can't be polite until I've had some breakfast," said Hern. "I'm frantic for it. We've eaten nothing but illusions since we landed. Isn't that so, Robin?"

"I don't think so. How should *I* know?" Robin said as she climbed into the boat.

We poled out from among the reeds into the current of the two rivers and went drifting down a reddish, lazy flood between two lines of trees that ought to have marked the banks. The bread was horribly stale. The cabbages smelled. We chewed carrots, tough cheese, and dried fruit. Duck was so hungry he ate an onion. His eyes streamed. We all felt soggy, irritable, and frightened in a gloomy sort of way. We knew we were back in real life, and we wished we knew the reasons for it: why Tanamil had kept us and why he had turned us out.

"You said we ate illusions," I said to Hern as we finished eating. "But you don't believe in enchantments."

"I believe in what I can see," said Hern. "I saw what happened to Gull. I damn near broke the spell, too. I wish I had. And that food was too good to be real. I can't accept it wasn't real, but I suppose I've got to. It's—it's offensive."

"Bad luck," Duck said politely.

Hern was too gloomy to hit him. He said, "It's the way it's all mixed up in my head that annoys me. I can't remember properly." I saw Hern was having the same trouble as me. "It's maddening!" he said. "Robin, what happened to us?"

"How should I know?" said Robin. She was gloomiest of the lot.

We put the sail up. There were worms, earwigs,

and beetles in the folds of the sail, and wood lice and things with many legs making their home under the mast. Hern scowled at them. He scowled at the trees as we beat slowly from line to line of them, tacking against the wind. We did not sail beyond the trees, although there were acres of white water, glittering into the distance beyond, because we did not know how deep it was. There were no people, only trees sticking up from sheets of water.

Hern said, "Does anything strike you about these trees?"

Nothing did. Duck said, as we sailed under spreading branches, "Oaks, elms, willows."

"Go back to sleep!" said Hern. "Tanaqui, you're supposed to notice things. What about these trees?"

I looked up. The oak we were under was large, but quite ordinary. It was just beginning to get leaves, like bundles of yellow rags. The elm and the willows beyond it were just as ordinary, because they were already bright new green. "Everyone knows oaks are late," I said. "Trees always look like this in Spring."

"That's it!" Hern shouted. "Exactly! When we came to the watersmeet, all the trees were bare!" We stared up at the new leaves, astonished. Hern was right. I remembered I had said it was like sailing back to winter, this far down the River. "Now think back to last night," Hern said. "There was a moon. But there was no moon when we set out, was there?"

That was true again. "What do you think has happened?" I said, shivering.

Hern scowled. "A lot of days have passed. I wish I knew how many. I wish I knew why. What was Tanamil up to?"

"Do you think he's made us . . . too late for—for the One's fire?" I said.

If any read my weaving and do not know the One, I must tell you that once a year, as soon as the floods go down in Spring, the One requires to be put in a fire, from which he emerges renewed. It is a peculiar habit, but he is the One and not like the other Undying. I do not know what would happen if the One went into his fire at the wrong time. No one has dared try it.

Hern hunched up and brooded. There was the chalky bleakness in his eyes that always frightens me. My brother Hern is going to be a frightening man if he grows up as angry as he is now. The stoop of his shoulders and the jut of his nose put me in mind of the shadow Uncle Kestrel cast on our wall. Hern stared out chalk-eyed over the white water and said, "We have been taught that the One is our ancestor. We have also been told that Gull's soul could be used to pour out the virtue of our ancestor. We hear that Heathens have skill in this. We meet a Heathen, and strange things happen. It has always seemed to me that the One's habits are insane, until now. But if I believe what I saw happen to Gull, why should I not believe that the One himself is under attack now? The question is—"

"Do stop going on about it, Hern," Robin said. "You must have noticed the days were going by."

"—are the floods going down?" said Hern.

"We didn't notice," I said. "Do you know how long we were there?"

"I didn't count," Robin said. "It felt about ten days."

"Ten days!" I exclaimed. "No wonder the cabbages were bad!"

"Are the floods going down or not?" said Hern.

We looked anxiously at the spreading waters. The River, in its double strength, was bringing down sticks, straw, boughs, leaves, and weed, between the two lines of trees. "Look, look!" Duck cried out, pointing to the nearest floating bough. We looked and found that it was moving not down the River but gently *backward*. We were aghast.

"The River's flowing the wrong way!" said Robin.

For over an hour the sticks, straw, and leaves continued to move gently upstream. Our boat still went forward, tacking against the wind, but we were all in the greatest panic. Duck and I hung over the side watching the debris. We had no idea if this meant the end of the floods or more malign magic.

"That magician by the sea must be turning the whole River now," I said.

"If there *is* a magician there," said Hern. "Think who told us there was." He stared at a place where the water was gently troubled, as if the true current of the River were forcing its way against the unnatural flow. "Gull's soul is one thing," he said. "It can't be very heavy. But it would take magic stronger than I can believe in to turn all this weight of water. There must be some other explanation."

To our surprise and relief, the sticks and weeds turned at midmorning and began going the proper way.

We stayed in the boat all that day. There was nowhere to land in the sheets of water on either side of the trees. But at nightfall we were all sick of raw food. In the dusk we saw what we took for a low island or small mountain out in the flood. We drew up the keel and poled cautiously across to it. It proved to be the roofs of a mighty house, not high, but covering the space of several cornfields. Some roofs were old thatch, some new and steep, of slippery tiles, with painted carvings at the ridge and bundles of tall chimneys.

"I bet the King lived here," said Duck.

We thought Duck was right. But everyone there had gone to the wars and not come back. We tied the boat to the bars of a window and landed on a flat space of tiles, bringing our Undying with us. Hern thought we might have to put the One in his fire anytime. I could not bear to touch Gull for many days after that, so I brought the Young One. As I set him down, I was struck by the resemblance between them. Gull seems to be made of the same flaky pink stone. Yet I know the Young One was carved many lifetimes ago.

There was only a glimmer of fire in both firepots. We tore off gilded carvings and red and blue rails from the roofs and used handfuls of thatch for kindling. Our fire smoked and smelled bad on the tiles, and smoke spread over the flat water.

After supper we left Robin sitting by the fire with her hands wrapped round the knees of her awful blue skirt and scrambled over the roofs in the near dark. I kept wishing I could see into the drowned rooms underneath. But I had to imagine the grandeur. Hern and I collided coming round the tall chimneys above our boat. While we were laughing, we heard the slop and creak of our boat swinging round to face upstream.

"It's happened again!" said Hern.

We slithered down the steep roof, and sure enough, we could see the boat turned and the rubbish from our supper drifting the wrong way. We knelt with our heads hanging off the roof, trying to see how fast the current went. Hern took a stick and held it with his fingers just out of the water.

"It can't be the end of the floods," he said. "My thumb's wet now."

Somebody laughed on the roof behind us. I thought it was Duck and turned to tell him about the current. But it was a Heathen girl. I could see just enough to know that she was fair-haired and not Robin. I nudged Hern and he looked, too.

"Er—good evening," we said. I don't know how Hern felt, but I was hoping very hard she would think we were Heathens too.

"Hallo," she said. "Why are you two making such a fuss about the tide?"

"Tide?" we said, stupid as owls in a strong light.

"You must know about it," she said. "The sea rises twice a day and comes up the River."

"Oh, we know all about that," Hern said. "We—er—we were just seeing how high it came up."

"Of course," she said.

"We know it's different by the sea," I lied.

"Of course," she said. I know she was laughing at us as she slipped away behind the chimneys.

We felt very foolish and very scared. When Robin and Duck learned we were sharing the roofs with Heathens, they wanted to row away in the dark, but we gave up that idea because we could not see where the two lines of trees were by then. Instead we threw our fire into the water and got into the boat. There we did not sleep for a long time, but we never heard a sound from the Heathens.

:∥ 7 ∥:

WE DID NOT HEAR the Heathens go, but we were the only people on the roofs in the morning. Hern and I climbed a tower in the middle and made sure of it.

"Now, please," said Robin as we were all getting into the boat, "let's decide where to stop. What kind of place do we want to live in?"

"We're going down to the sea first," said Duck.

"Surely not," Robin said. She gestured to the pink clay brother in the bows of the boat. "Think of Gull."

At once it was certain that Duck, Hern, and I were all settled on going to the sea. "I do think of Gull," said Hern. "I want to see that magician—if there *is* a magician. I'm going to flood him out with real things. I shan't believe a word he says. That's the only way to deal with magic."

"I'd have thought more magic would be better," said Duck. "But I've got to go there, too."

My thought was that we would find a magician by the sea and he would prove to be Tanamil. I growled like a dog, I was so angry—angry with Tanamil and angry with myself for believing anything he said. "I'm going to see that magician," I said, "and I'm going to rescue Gull." I knew I had not the power to do that. I took up the One and shook him, I was so angry. "He'll help," I said. "He'd better!"

"Tanaqui!" said Robin. "You mustn't threaten the Undying! I think you're all mad or—or something."

"Don't you start on about being the eldest and knowing best!" said Hern. "We've all decided."

"I wasn't," Robin protested. "I don't know best. I don't know anything anymore. All I know is that it's dangerous. If I didn't know it was quite as dangerous in Shelling, I'd ask to go home." She bent her head, and tears dripped. Hern sighed.

"We'll find a really nice home when we've been to the sea, Robin," I said.

It took us four days to come near the sea. It might have taken longer if the wind had not backed to south-west and come hurling over the plains of water, bringing ruffles like gooseflesh. With that we made speed even when the tide turned and flowed up the River. Each day it flowed more strongly, until we came to expect it, as we expected the sun to rise. We found it useful, for it showed us where the River truly ran.

There were no more trees to mark the River after the first day. Instead there was a very confusing landscape.

I think more people had lived in that part of the land than I knew existed before. It rose into humps and lumps everywhere. The flooded River flowed round them in lakes, in strings of shallow pools, and in a multitude of smaller rivers. Often the first sign we had that we had missed the main River was that we found ourselves sailing beside the posts of a fence. There were houses on nearly every hump of land and more houses half underwater. Not all these houses were burned, but there were no people anywhere. We risked staying in an empty house one night, but none of us felt comfortable there. Even when we put our Undying in the empty niches by the hearth, it still felt like someone else's house.

Many of the humps had animals on them. We have three cats now, Rusty, and Ratchet, and Sweetheart, who came from the island where the gulls were. I love cats. Robin named them. There was one island full of dogs, but they were wild and hungry and barked at us so fiercely that we did not go near them. Most of the humps were full of sheep. They had lambs, because it was Spring. We wondered whether to catch some to eat, but we were not that hungry yet. We had plenty of dried fruit and pickled fish, and there were cows stranded on every hillside. Once we had got used to the way things were, we did not hesitate to milk those cows.

By the fourth evening in that confusing landscape, the mountains we kept seeing in the distance drew in around us, in the form of low, empty-looking hills. They were dark, stony, and infertile. But the island we landed on was grassy and covered with bushes. There little black Sweetheart came running to meet us, purring and mewing. Never have I seen a cat more glad to have human company.

That morning I was woken by melancholy crying. I got up and found the waters covered with white floating birds, and more flying, catching the sun in a way that had me blinking.

"What are these large mournful birds?" I said.

Hern laughed. "Haven't you seen seagulls before?"

"She may not have done," Robin said. "They stopped coming to Shelling years ago. They used to come and cover the field when it was plowed, Tanaqui, and Father said they came inland to get away from the Spring storms."

"But I remember them," Hern protested. "She's only a year younger than me."

"Please, Hern," said Robin. "I'm much too tired to quarrel about seagulls."

"They used to come after the floods," Hern said. "Does that mean the River's going down, then?" He scrambled to test the height of the water. He tried a different way nearly every day to see if the floods were over, but the tides grew stronger and steeper the nearer we came to the sea and defeated all his methods. That day Hern hung a piece of twine with knots in it from a bush. But the end of it floated instead of sinking, and Sweetheart came along and played with it. Hern roared at her. It was very odd: Hern, of all of us, was the one who was determined that the One should go in his fire at the proper time.

Duck picked Sweetheart up. "Don't make such a fuss, Hern," he said. "When the floods go down, it'll be quite obvious."

"But we don't have a bank to measure by!" Hern snarled.

"Then we'll find out some other way," said Duck.

"Stop maddening me," said Hern. "Take that cat away."

Robin was very quiet as we sailed that morning. I should have noticed she was not well, I know, but I was thinking of other things. The gulls followed us. They made a noise like sharp misery, and I was afraid of them. They watched us with hungry eyes like beads. When they floated on the River, they seemed lighter than was natural. I was not sure they were really birds. There was a new light in the air, bleached and chalky, like bones, or Hern's eyes when he is angry, and the gulls wheeled about in it. The hills on either side of us were low and rocky, with no trees to speak of, and they seemed to come together in front of us into a bank of mist. The wind hissed over them. The River filled the wide space in between, gray now, and covered with angry shivers in all directions. Where the water met the land, it rose into high waves with white tops. These waves went riding landward, growing taller as they rode, until they were too tall for themselves, whereupon the white top fell over and smashed on the land. Everywhere was crash, crash of falling waves, and the seagulls crying out. I kept looking at Gull to make sure he was safe. I was frightened.

Hern and Duck became frightened, too, when we found we were not masters of the boat any longer. None of us understands the mass of contradictory currents in which the water flowed to the sea. Sometimes we were racing forward, sometimes we seemed hardly to move, and then, around midday, we were taken by the tide and borne back toward Sweetheart's island. We kept the sail up and tried to beat on, but we found we were taken more and more toward the left. After a whole morning we had gone barely two miles.

"I think we'd better keep leftward," Hern said at last, "and try to land somewhere over there."

"Oh, yes, do let's land!" Robin said. She said it so desperately that we all looked at her and saw that she was ill. She was shivering, and her face was an odd color—almost like the lilac flowers in Aunt Zara's garden. I think we did wrong to bring Robin to the sea.

Hern said, "I'll land in the first possible place."

Duck picked up a blanket and wrapped it round Robin. "Would you like the Lady, Robin?" he said. I confess now that I felt jealous at how kind they both were to Robin. I found it hard to be kind to her, and I still do. She looked so ugly, and she kept shivering for no reason. I hope I did not show my feelings. I put the Lady in Robin's hands, but Robin seemed to forget her, and she dropped to the boards.

"Have the Young One," said Duck.

"No," Robin said, with great firmness.

After endless sailing in heaving gray water, we came near land. It would be midafternoon by then. Everything was bleached, brownish, and sandy-looking and smelling a new smell, like a fresh-caught fish. That is the smell of the sea. And the land was not in a solid line as we had thought, but in islands of heaped-up sand, with the true land just as sandy, some way beyond. In between the land and the islands the sand-colored water raced and sucked, while on the outer side of them it was all waves, crashing continually. How Hern got us ashore on the last island, I shall never know. He must be a better boatman than me.

Here was our final island. It was made of crusty sand. Sharp-edged grass grew on it and bent prickly bushes, all twisted in the wind. The wind had dug out holes and hollows in the sand. We found the largest hollow, facing back to the land we had come from—from there it looked like blue mountains—and we made a camp, dragging the boat up to give Robin some shelter. Down below was a place where all the things in that part of the flood were hurled on the island and pinned there by the racing water.

"Ugh!" said Duck when he saw it.

There were dead hens, drowned rats, cabbage stalks—many horrid remains—but there was wood and waterweed, too. We made a good fire from it. We wrapped Robin in rugcoats and blankets, and she still shivered. We offered her food.

"I couldn't!" she said. "Just water."

"Water!" I said. Hern and I looked at one another. There was a drop in the jar, but there was no water on the island. I went down to the gray flood and tasted it. The River here mingles with the sea, and the sea is salt. I do not know where the salt comes from, but the sea is not fit to drink.

"What do we do now?" I whispered.

"We can't take the boat," Hern whispered back. "She'd be cold without it, and the current's terrible. I can't see any sign of a stream either."

We gazed at the low sandy land helplessly. Naturally Duck chose that moment to say in a loud voice, "I'm dreadfully thirsty!"

"Shut up!" we both said.

But there was Robin heaving herself up on one arm, with rugs dropping from her and her teeth chattering in her blue-gray mouth. "Is the water gone? I'll go and get—"

"You lie down," I said, glaring at Duck. "I'm just going to get some." I took the water jar and stumped off up the sandy hill, with no idea what I was going to do. I was really depressed. When I come to think of it, I find wide-open spaces always make me unhappy. It was the same with the lake. I have been brought up where the land is hilly and close. Here it was as if the land had not been properly made. Everything was flat and sand gray or River gray and hung with peculiar purple-gray mist. You could not see very far, even if there was anything to see. The only thing my eye could cling to was the wide channel of rushing gray water between me and the shore, and I did not see myself getting across that.

All the same, I stumped down toward the channel. I had some notion that the water would not be salty there. And as I went, I thought I heard Duck screaming from the rushing channel. It was the way he screams when he is really frightened. "Help!" he screamed.

I remember I dropped the jar and came down to the water like a plow in a furrow of dry sand. It was not Duck. It was a much smaller child. He was in the channel, thrashing about in the racing muddy water and traveling past in it as fast as I could walk, screaming all the while. There was a horrid while when I seemed to stand there staring. But I think I took my shoes off and got out of my rugcoat while I stared.

"Keep swimming!" I screamed at the child. "Swim for your life!" He heard me. A fountain of water went up from his arms and legs, but I could see he had no idea how to swim. I plowed down into the water. I remember squawking. It was far colder than the River is by Shelling, and the bottom was no bottom at all. It was just sinking stuff. You had to swim or sink in the mud. I swam madly. I had never swum in a flood before. My father forbade it. But I think, even that first night of the flood, the current was not as strong as the one in that race. My legs were towed sideways before I was afloat. No wonder the child screamed so. I swam with my whole strength, and yet I could not seem to cross that narrow channel.

I think I caught up with that drowning child simply from being heavier. Since I was trying to go forward, I was carried to him on a slant. That is, I was carried to where I had last seen him. He had gone down a second time by then. I thought he was drowned, and I was thinking of saving myself when a heavy sand-colored head bobbed up just by my fingers. I wound my hand in the hair and pulled.

Then it was all panic. The child's terror got into me, too. We both thrashed and screamed and sank. I roared at him to be quiet, and he shrilled at me to let go, and to get him out, and called me names. I called him a crab-faced idiot and fought him until the water was in spouts round us. While we struggled, the current dragged us along against the land, and I saw we were traveling out toward the sea. I put my hand against the bank to stop us. And my hand stuck in the land, up to my elbow. I dream of that still. The bank was as soft as curd cheese. Somehow, I got us out onto it, out of the sucking waters, and the cheeselike land sucked us down instead. I floundered through it, dragging that poor child by his hair. I came to hard sand under my elbows, coarse as sugar, and I cried with relief.

The child cried, too, on hands and knees, with water

pouring out of his mouth and hair. His face was red and blue in patches, and his bare feet and legs were raw purple. He was wearing a silly kind of tunic and drawers which must have been cold even when he was dry. He shivered, and I shook.

"Shut up," I said. "You're all right now." He looked at me as if it was all my fault. "You're saved," I said. "By me. You're looking at the person who pulled you out. How did you fall in, anyway?" He seemed vague about that. He muttered something. "I see," I said. "You were fooling about and you slipped. Where do you live?"

He gave me a shifty look. I think he said, "I didn't say that," but he still didn't speak properly.

"Then what did you say?" I said.

"I said some natives pushed me in." He said it very loudly and clearly, so there was no mistake, and he gave me the defiant look people do when they are lying.

"Liar," I said, but I said it without thinking. The wretched child was a Heathen. My wet hair was the same sand color as his, and I knew his would dry fair, too. I thought that if I had let him drown, it would have been revenge for my father at least, but what had my father to do with him? I could not have stood on the island and let him drown. "You'd better go home and get into dry clothes," I said. "Where can I find some water?"

He gave me another sideways look and pointed to the racing channel behind us.

"Very funny!" I said. "Do you think I'm a fool?" He shook his head swiftly. "Water to drink," I said. "I was looking for some when I heard you yelling."

He looked at me from the corners of his eyes, very carefully. Maybe he knew I was not a Heathen. Something made him afraid and respectful of me. "There's water up here," he said, and jerked his shivering chin to the sandy hill above us.

"Show me," I said.

Both shivering hugely, we marched up and inland, over one sandy hump and round another. The wind was cruel. And there, running between two more sand-humps, was a peculiar little stream, very flat and shallow. It came out of the sand about a foot above my head and, instead of flowing down into the River, simply buried itself in the sand and vanished, just beside my mauve feet. I tasted it, and it was good. "Thanks," I said. "Now you've shown me, you can go home, but mind you tell them the truth about what happened. If you spin them that story about the natives pushing you in, I shall know at once, and I shall come and get you." I did not see why he should blame our people for his own silliness.

"All right," he muttered, pushing at the sand with his poor sore toes. I could see I had impressed him. He was a lot younger than Duck.

"Good," I said. "Off you go, then."

He was gone, in a shower of sand, before I finished saying it. He never said thank you. He was a very ungrateful, very Heathen brat.

I knelt beside the stream for a while, playing with its peculiarities. I have since learned that such streams are common at the Rivermouth, but I had never seen anything like it. Dig as I might, I could not find where it came from. Then I noticed that I was freezing cold and that I had no way of carrying the water. I got up and went lumbering on my frozen legs until I could see our island.

It was some way up the shore from me. I could see Duck and Hern bending anxiously over the plowed place where I had gone into the channel.

"Hey!" I shouted. "Where's the water jar?"

Both their heads jerked up. I laughed. They looked out to sea first, expecting me to be there. That was really stupid of them because while I had been digging at the stream, the tide had turned and the water in the channel was rushing inland again. The whole channel was smaller, shallower, and more gentle.

Duck ran away to fetch the jar. Hern tried to yell at me about how I had crossed the channel, and I tried to shriek back about the Heathen brat, but neither of us heard much for the wind. Then Duck came galloping back down the island with the water jar and galloped straight to the water. I suddenly saw he was going to try to cross it.

"Stop!" I screamed at him, remembering the sinking bottom. "I'm wet already." If I had told him about the mud and the current, that would not have stopped him. I ran into the channel myself instead. My feet sank, but nothing like as badly as they had done before.

The water came up to my knees—I was so cold by then that it felt warm—and then up to my waist, but that was all. The current was not fierce at all. I could hardly believe it.

"What was the fuss about? I could have come over easily," Duck pointed out when I got to the other side.

"I told you—I'm wet already," I said. I took the jar and waded back. This time the water hardly reached the top of my legs. I shall never understand tides, I said to myself.

When I came back with the full jar, the channel had narrowed again. It was a brisk stream of salt water, which came just to my knees in the middle. On either side of it were wide places of brown sand, but I did not sink in them above my ankles. I could hear it, *trickle-trickle*, *smicker-smicker*, as the water drained from it, and worms were wriggling up under my toes.

Hern took the jar from me. "Lucky the tide's running out."

"It isn't," I said. "It's running up-River."

"Then why is it so low?" said Duck.

At that we all said at once, "The floods are going down!" It was a great relief to find Tanamil had not made us miss the One's fire after all.

"What a shame Robin's ill for it," said Duck.

"There are Heathen near," I said. "Should we make a fire? I pulled a Heathen brat out of the water."

"It can't be helped," said Hern. His head went pecking forward, as it does when he is determined. "I'm not going to let any Heathen, magicians or otherwise, interfere with what the One thinks is due to him. Let's get some firewood."

It has to be a special fire for the One, newly kindled from our hearth. Usually we do it on the bank of the River near our house. As I went shivering to the camp with the water, I hoped the One would not find it too strange when he came out of his fire on this miserable island. Usually, too, we celebrate with a feast, but I knew there was no question of feasting this time, even before I saw Robin.

Robin was worse. She was shivering as badly as I was, but she had thrown off the blankets and taken off most of her clothes. She said she was too hot. "I'm so thirsty!" she said.

I gave her a long drink and made her get under the blankets again. She would not put on her clothes. She had thrown them up the hill and the cats were lying on them. "Well, if you won't wear them," I said, "I will. I'm soaked." I was so frozen by then that I could not bear to unpack all the lockers in the boat to find my own clothes. I put on Robin's underclothes and her awful blue skirt. My rugcoat was dry, of course, so I put that on, and my shoes. The cats came and sat on the skirt again, with me in it, which helped me to get warm. But Robin still shivered. She looked uglier than ever.

"I'm sore all over," she said.

"You've got the River fever again," I said. "It won't last long."

"Where are the boys?" she said.

"Gull's in the boat," I said. "Hern and Duck are getting wood for the One. The floods are going down."

Robin sprang up again. "Oh, I must see to it! They'll never get it right!"

"Lie down," I said. "They can do it here where you can see them, and you can tell them what to do. But I'll tell them not to do it at all if you get up." I am like that with Robin all the time—not kind. I try to be patient, but she is far more annoying ill than well.

Hern and Duck came back with loads of wood. They had pulled up the thick-branched prickle bushes from all over the island. They were determined to make it a good fire, in spite of the situation. They dug a flat shelf out of the sand above the camp and built the wood up there as Robin told them. We took a long time and did it really well.

When it was ready, Hern, as head of the family, took the One from the boat and put him in the niche we had made in the center of the wood. The One looked just as usual, dark and rigid, and covered with small glisters. It was hard to believe that he knew what was happening. Robin sat up between Duck and me while Hern lit the wood with a coal from our firepot.

We all said, "May the clay purge from you. Come forth again in your true strength."

This is what we always say. Then we watched the flames roar up in the wind. Our campfire was dwarfed. In that light, wide space the flames looked pale and saw-edged. The One was soon lost in them. They raced up from the edge of the hill, whirling round and round, and dropped flaming pieces on the water.

We were staring at the blaze, thinking that it was the best fire we had ever made, when we heard shouts.

"What was that?" said Robin.

"Hey there! You on the island!"

"I'll go," said Hern. Naturally Duck and I went over the hill with him.

On the shore opposite, beyond the small stream that was all that was left of the racing channel, a row of Heathen men were standing.

"Hey you!" they shouted. "Come over here!"

:‖ 8 ‖:

AT FIRST I THOUGHT the Heathen were monstrously tall, with strange-shaped heads. Then I saw that they had on iron hats which came high in the crown. The strange shapes were decorations made of feathers and tufts of fur and colored tassels. They had tunics like the Heathen brat's, but they wore long boots and gauntlets and flapping heavy cloaks, which made the outfit look a little warmer. They were all strong, strapping men. Three of them leaned on spears. The other two carried what looked like short planks with a little bow on one end. We knew those were the bows Uncle Kestrel told us of, which could send a bolt through two men at once.

"The fire gave us away," said Hern. "Pretend we're Heathens, too."

"How can we?" I said. "With the One in his fire."

"Shut up!" said Hern. The Heathen were shouting to us again to come over to them. "Why should we?" Hern shouted back. "What do you want?"

Several of them shouted back and beckoned. We could not hear what they said. "Are they talking about a King?" Duck said. The confused shouting and the beckoning continued, but none of the Heathen tried to cross the channel. They thought, as I had done, that it was still sinking mud there. As we still stood there, the two with bows pointed them at us.

"I think," said Hern, "we'd better do what they want. Tanaqui, go and tell Robin to lie low and look after the One. Don't upset her."

They hoped to cross over to the Heathen while I talked to Robin. I would never have forgiven them for that. But when I went back over the hill, Robin was asleep with the cats curled up round her, and the One's fire was blazing majestically. I threw some wood on the campfire and raced back. I was in time to catch Hern and Duck as they walked into the water. I bunched up Robin's skirt and splashed after them.

The Heathens were taller than I thought. They wore iron waistcoats, which looked even odder than the hats. All of them had brown skins and long noses like Hern's, and from below the metal hats tumbled hair that was either fair as ours or the brown color of the sand. They stared at us with as much interest as we stared at them.

"Just as Ked said!" one of them remarked. "Who

would have thought it! Tell me, your honors, which of you pulled a lad from the waters awhile back?" The Heathen accent is hard to understand. Their voices lift in all the wrong places. That was why I had not been able to understand the Heathen brat very well. You have to listen hard, as if you were deaf.

"Er—that was me," I said.

The Heathen raised frosty eyebrows at me. He had a very grizzled and important look. "The lad said it was a youth."

"I was wearing my brother's clothes," I explained.

"She was soaking, and she had to change," said Duck.

"If you think it's important," said Hern.

The Heathens heard us attentively, with strained frowns. I think they found us hard to follow, too. "It is important, your honors," said the grizzled one, "if I am to take the right one to the King." Then he gave an apologizing kind of cough. "Will it trouble you all three to come with us?"

It was strange that he was so polite. It ought to have made me much less frightened. But the men with the bows remained tense and alert, holding an arrow ready to fire and glancing from us to the land around all the time. Looking back, I think maybe that it was not us they intended to shoot.

Hern was very good all through. He did not understand what the man asked straightaway, but he made it seem as if he was considering. "We shall be pleased to see your King," he said, and pecked with his head, graciously.

"This way," said the Heathen. He turned and walked off. Another spear-carrier stepped in front of him, releasing his spear from his cloak. The spear proved to hold a flag full of all sorts of colored devices. We walked behind him over the sandy hills, feeling like part of the Shelling River Procession. I had only seen a flag used for religion before, but this one, as it clapped to and fro over our heads, held no religious picture that I could see.

It was not very far, onto higher land and crustier sand, where grew a stand of trees all bent as if to hold their backs to the sea. There, by another sandy river, was a collection of dwellings no larger than Shelling. As Duck said later, it would have frightened us to death if we had known our camp was so near the King of the Heathens—always supposing we had noticed the King's camp when we saw it. It was of tattered tents and driftwood huts, with rubbish thrown about. It was poor beside the poorest village I have seen since. Yet more flags flew from the rickety roofs as proudly and religiously as you please.

"What kind of King have we come to?" Hern said out of the corner of his mouth.

Duck and I did not feel so scornful. The bowmen could shoot us here as easily as in a palace.

The grizzled Heathen stepped into one of the tattered tents. We waited outside with the flag and the crossbows. Since it was a tent, we could hear what was said inside amid the rattling of the canvas. But we had difficulty understanding it.

I heard, "I have brought no less than three young mages, lord, not knowing quite what else to do." There followed talk I could not hear for the tent flapping. Then, "I think Ked told the truth for once, lord. I find them very hard to understand, and by their dress, they seem to have gone native." After this they spoke so rapidly that I was lost, until the messenger said, "I agree, lord. It may be just what you were wanting."

Meanwhile, we stood feeling slighted and uneasy. We did not know why the King should want us. We thought of Gull and of Tanamil. And we found it ominous that though there were numbers of Heathens about in the camp, they did not come crowding to see us, as people would have done in Shelling. I saw that women and girls kept quietly slipping across behind us to the sandy river, where they fetched water in iron pots. They could not all have wanted water at once. It was an excuse to see us. They were none of them as pretty as Robin, but I liked their clinging dresses. Men and boys were finding excuses to be about, too. Someone tidied a heap of rubbish. Someone came past with a tall horse. A boy staggered with a sack from one hut to another, and so on. We were being seen secretly all the time we waited, and it made us most uncomfortable.

At last the messenger came out and held the flap of

the tent for us. "Please go in. My lord is waiting for you."

By this time we were used to the speech. We went in, all of us thinking of Gull and very suspicious. The King stood up to meet us. That was a politeness. But Duck had his mind so firmly on Gull that he said, "No one here's going to take *my* soul."

"I think you know more about that than I do," the King said politely. "Let me assure you that there is no question of that."

He was no older than Gull and not as tall as Hern. We stared at him awkwardly, and he at us. He was really very like Hern, except that he had a slender, unhealthy look, and I think he walked with a limp, though I am not too sure of this, because he was sitting down most of the time. Hern looked surprisingly tall and sturdy beside him. Hern, I am sure, has grown inches since we left Shelling. But they both had the same forward set of the head and the same sharp nose, and they both knew it, too. They looked at one another with strong interest—that interest which can be friendship or hatred at the drop of a pin.

"I am Kars Adon," this thin young King said, "son of Kiniren. The clans owe allegiance to me now my father is dead." He was not boasting when he said this. He spoke as facts, to let us know who he was. I marveled that he named himself Adon. It is one of the secret names of our One, and we do not say it openly. He added, "Perhaps you would like to sit down," and smiled awkwardly at us, before sitting down himself in a folding chair of studded leather and wood.

That chair was not fine, but it was the only good thing in the tent. In front of it, someone had arranged a tree stump, a milking stool, and a wicker basket. Hern sat on the milking stool, which I knew was a politeness because it put him lower than Kars Adon. Duck took the basket, and I sat gingerly on the stump. It rocked rather.

"Tell me," I said, "does your name have a meaning?" Kars Adon followed our speech well. "No," he said, with only a small pause. "It is just a name. Why?"

"Our names mean things," Duck explained. "I am Mallard, he is Hern, and she is Tanaqui. Our father was Closti the Clam."

I could see Kars Adon found this quite outlandish, but he was too polite to say so. "I am of Rath Clan, like Ked," he said, and seemed to look at us expectantly. "I must thank you for rescuing Ked from the River," he said. "I am deeply in your debt."

He meant it. From what he said, I thought the brat must be his brother. "It was nothing," I said, and I did not say what an ungrateful little beast he was. "Is he a near relation of yours?"

"I don't think so," Kars Adon said uncertainly. "He belongs to my clan, of course. But even if he didn't, I'd be grateful. There are so few of us now—" He sighed, but it seemed as if he felt it wrong to be sad. He sat up straight and smiled at us. "What Ked said when he came back made me decide to send for you," he said. "Forgive me. I know you mages are not subject to orders. But Ked swore that the person who rescued him had power to walk on the greediest waters and not only snatched him from the River's mouth but bound him to tell the truth about it. And when Arin fetched you, he saw with his own eyes all three of you walk where he would have been sucked down, and he knew that Ked had told the truth. And we all know," Kars Adon said seriously, "that anyone with power over that monstrous River is a mage indeed. Though I am inclined to think," he added, with a little twitch of a smile, "that forcing Ked to tell the truth shows greater power still."

I was getting truly uncomfortable. I could see Hern and Duck trying not to look at me and laugh. "I don't think we are mages," I said.

"Speak for yourself," Duck said, creaking on his basket. "Personally I have some quite uncanny powers." Sometimes Duck is as bad as Ked.

Kars Adon again looked at us expectantly, as if we were supposed to say something else. When we did not, he said, in an awkward way, as if he were having to remind us of a duty, "Before we go any further, you should tell me your clan and allegiances."

That was a bad moment. Duck and I did not know what to say. I half expected Hern to make up something since I could see he was in that kind of mood, but Hern still said nothing. The stump wobbled under me with my fear and shame. I was ashamed that Kars Adon should so confidently think we were Heathen like himself, and I was terrified he would find out we were not and kill us for it.

"Ked and Arin both said that your speech was strange and you dressed as natives do," Kars Adon said. "I can see that for myself. There are two things you could be." His face grew red under its Heathen brown as he said this. I think, by his standards, he was being very impolite. "You could be of a small Western clan, one of those who came here before we did. Forgive me. Or instead you are some of Kankredin's people." He thought he was being so rude that he could scarcely bear to look at us.

"Who is Kankredin?" said Duck.

Kars Adon was in quite a taking at this. He knew he had been rude, and he wanted to look away, but he was also so astonished that Duck had not heard of this Kankredin that he wanted to stare at Duck to see if Duck was pretending. Between looking and not looking, twisting his hands together, and fumbling at the clasp of his cloak, he made us feel quite as bad. "Kankredin," he said. "Kankredin is mage of mages. It is Kankredin in the ship beyond the sandbars. You must have seen the ship at least!"

Hern's head pecked forward at this. Duck said blandly—I never knew Duck was such a liar—"We suspected there was a ship there, but it was hidden in an enchanted mist."

"Yes, that is Kankredin," Kars Adon said eagerly. "We've been warned to keep clear of his mist. It was Kankredin I wanted to talk to you about. You see—"

"Just a moment," said Hern. "Before you go any further." Now Hern had not said a word up to then. He says he was absorbed in finding out what manner of person this Kars Adon was. "Before you say another word," he snapped out suddenly. And he jumped up from the stool and pounced to the opening of the tent. Kars Adon stared at Hern. This was real rudeness.

"Hern!" I said.

"Stand back there!" Hern said at the door of the tent, speaking very loud and slow. "I want to say something private to the King."

A great many voices made objection to this. I think everyone in the camp was standing there listening in.

"I know that," said Hern. "But you can guard him from where you can't hear. Get over near that hut, all of you."

There were more objections outside.

"What do you take us for?" said Hern. "We could have had the King to the top of the Black Mountains by now if we wanted. I swear to you we are not going to harm a hair of his head or a hair of his soul's head. But I must speak to the King alone. Now move away, all of you."

Feet shuffled off, from all round the tent. It must have been every Heathen in the place. Hern peeked a look round to make sure they had all gone, and then he came back inside. Kars Adon lifted his chin and gave him a haughty stare. I admired that. Kars Adon must have been afraid Hern was going to work all sorts of terrible enchantments on him, but he let Hern know who was King here. As for Hern, I could see him shaking at his own audacity. When he saw the King look, he went bright red.

"I apologize for that," he said, and sat on the stool again—I think his knees gave way. "I had to get them out of the way because I'm going to be frank with you, and I didn't want to be murdered on the spot. Before you tell us about Kankredin, I want to tell you that we are not of your people or of any clan of your people. We are natives, as you would say."

"Is it possible?" said Kars Adon. "You look as we do." He was really frightened now. So was I. When Hern launches himself on one of his rash ideas, you never know what will happen.

"My father's fathers," said Hern, "were born here by the River, as far back as I know. I wanted to tell you that, by way of friendship, and to prevent mistakes. Otherwise—well, you've already let us know there are not many of you, that your father is dead, that you're camped in a bad place without too much food, and in some trouble with Kankredin besides." This astonished me. But Hern was quite right. What Kars Adon had not told us, we could see by looking at his camp. "So before you give away all your plans and secrets," Hern said, "I shall have to tell you we are your enemies. If I didn't, we'd have given ourselves away somehow, and you'd have killed us, and we'd have lost our chance to help one another. Aren't I right?"

"I . . . suppose so," Kars Adon said. He looked at

Hern dubiously. He wanted to trust Hern, for whatever trouble he was in, but he was not sure at all. I did not blame him. I was not sure I trusted Hern either.

"So why did you send for us?" Hern asked.

"He probably doesn't want us anymore," said Duck. He thought Hern was mad.

"I think I do," said Kars Adon. "Only mages can understand a mage. I am sure you have the power to reach Kankredin in his ship. But I do not want to send enemies to him or tell you—" He did not seem to know what to say.

"Tell us as little as you can," I suggested.

"If this will help you," said Hern, "we were going to see Kankredin anyway. We just didn't know his name. And though we are your enemies by birth, our people do not love us. They think we are Heathens, too." It is hard to explain the bitterness with which Hern spoke. He must have been remembering Zwitt and Aunt Zara and Gull in anger for a long time. Kars Adon looked at him and wondered.

"What makes you a Heathen?" Duck asked Kars Adon.

"I don't know what you mean," Kars Adon said.

"Do you believe in the Undying?" I said.

Kars Adon smiled. "We've no use for dolls beside our fireplaces, if that's what you mean. The Undying are not clay figures. But when I die, I hope to be gathered to them."

This made me very indignant, but I could see, all

the same, that Kars Adon did in some manner believe in the Undying.

"I will tell you," Kars Adon said suddenly, "since you know so much already. Kankredin has been all the while out on his ship, wrestling with the might of your River. But when my father was killed, he knew, and sent one of his mages to bring us here, where he told us to stay. He promised us that he would conquer the land for us, through the River. But while we wait here, those of us who have not been killed by the natives are being sucked in by the River. The River is a greedy and devouring monster. It has carried off all our ships, except one. Kankredin has angered it with his enchantments, and it rises in ever-increasing might. And we suffer for it, not Kankredin."

It really might have been Zwitt or Aunt Zara talking. But Kars Adon evidently believed it.

"I have known for some time that we must leave," he said.

"Will you go away home?" I asked hopefully.

"That seems the only thing to do," Kars Adon said. "We must build another ship and go. Now that my father is dead, my uncle will let us come back; they had quarreled, you see. It means that I must give up all claim to the throne and perhaps have both hands cut off, but I owe it to my clans." He seemed very calm about this. "But," he added sadly, "Kankredin will not let us out through the Rivermouth for any reason. I want to ask you to make him let us go."

"Fair enough," said Hern. "But what do you really want to do?"

"What do I want?" Kars Adon said. He lifted his head and stared at the gray flapping wall of the tent. "I want to go inland and found my kingdom there, of course. It is a wide country. There is plenty of room for us and the natives. I think there are certainly scattered bands from the clans between here and the mountains. I shall call them in and make a city. I don't pretend it will be easy, but someday we shall be a great people again." The way he said this made me think of flags flying over stone roofs and golden towers, and I really believed he could do it.

"That's a bit hard on us natives," said Duck.

"I shall make treaties with you. If you choose to fight, I shall win," said Kars Adon, lost in high dreams.

"Right. When do you start?" said Hern.

That brought Kars Adon back to earth. He put his chin down and looked bleakly at Hern. Hern looked bleak and chalky back. The windy air in the tent seemed full of flags and half-heard trumpets out of Kars Adon's thoughts.

"You want me to go to Kankredin and get his permission for you to conquer the country?" Hern asked, in his most jeering way.

Kars Adon was so angry that he stood up and took a limping step toward Hern. "I am not the servant of any mage!"

Hern stood up too, showing himself again much

larger—not that this daunted Kars Adon. "That's more like it," Hern said. "Then what's keeping you here?"

Kars Adon glared at Hern. "The River. The River drowns anyone who tries to go inland. Tell Kankredin from me that he must leave the River alone."

"I shall do that with pleasure," said Hern. "We've already spoken to the River. You'll find the waters are going down." He could not stop himself from smiling as he said this.

Kars Adon smiled, too. He was so pleased that he put out a damp knuckly hand and wrung each of our hands in turn. "Thank you," he said. "I wish I could offer you a reward or something to eat or drink, but—" He paused a little blankly. I think the Heathen notion of gratitude was to shower food and drink on people, and possibly gold and silver, too, and it seemed to hurt Kars Adon that he could not do it. "I give my protection and friendship freely to all three of you," he said, rather lamely. "I suppose you'll go to Kankredin when the tide starts running out?"

It was lucky he said that. We still had no notion about the tides. I turned to Hern and said knowingly, "Now, the tide turns when?"

"Um," said Hern, pulling his chin wisely.

"It'll be around sunrise tomorrow," Kars Adon said obligingly, "won't it?" He knew all about tides. His people came from the sea. It was odd that he knew so little of the River.

"We'll set off at sunrise," Duck said, as wise as Hern.

"And so will we," Kars Adon said eagerly. "I shall

have them strike camp tonight." His flags and trumpets were back. "We should be many miles inland by tomorrow night," he said.

After that we said good-bye with great politeness and went back to our island. Arin and his flag bearer did not come beyond the edge of the camp with us. They were too anxious to get back and find out what had been said. That was fortunate, because when we reached the channel, no one would have believed Ked and I had nearly drowned in it. It was nothing but a ditch of wet brown sand. They would have known we were not mages.

We could see the One's fire flaring beyond the hill of our island. "I hope Robin's all right," said Hern.

"And the One," I said. "Hern, what got into you?"

"I could see he liked straight dealing," said Hern. "And I took a risk. I wanted to find out about this Kankredin. And we did. I'm going to give him a piece of my mind tomorrow."

"But," I said, "you've sent him off—Kars Adon and his Heathens—to get slaughtered inland. Just those few of them can never last."

"We've done our people a service," Duck said complacently.

But Hern said, as we trod across the brown ditch, leaving pale footprints, "It was better than sitting on a sandhill dreaming dreams. If I was him, I'd never have gone there in the first place."

:‖ 9 ‖:

SUNRISE NEXT DAY came with a fine itching mist of rain. I was woken by miserable wet cats trying to get under my blankets. My clothes, which I had hung on the boat to dry, were wet as ever, and Robin, while she was no worse, was not better. And in spite of the rain, the One's fire was by no means out. It had fallen inward to a flat heap of charcoal, in which blackness and redness came and went as the rain met it, but it was as hot as it was the night before.

This was a serious difficulty. When the One is newly out of his fire, he is at his strongest, and I knew we should take him with us to meet Kankredin. The One signifies that he is ready to come out by putting the fire out and appearing among the ashes. He was not ready. We argued about what we should do. The argument was made more urgent by the sound of the tide racing seaward on three sides of us.

Hern said, "There's no need for anyone to go but me. You two aren't reasonable enough, anyway."

Duck and I refused to stay behind. Duck said he had bound himself to go, too. I wanted to confront Tanamil. "And suppose you're not back when the One is ready to come out?" I said. It had to be Hern, as head of the family, who took the One from the fire.

Then Hern suggested pouring water on the fire and taking the One out at once. That is Hern all over. I would not hear of it. Neither would Robin. By this time Robin had realized what we were intending to do. She started croaking—her voice had become like a raven's, as ugly as her face—on and on at us that we were not to go out to sea, that Mother would not like it, that we were not to go without her, and a dozen other objections beside.

She annoyed me. I am sure the reason we are stuck in this old mill, having failed at everything, is that I got so annoyed with Robin that morning. We should have waited until the One was ready to go with us. The Lady and the Young One were not strong enough alone. But I still think we were right not to take Robin. I do not think her soul would have been safe.

I jumped up. "Let's go," I said to Hern. "If the One doesn't want to come, it's his bad luck. He can stay with Robin." Robin sat up, with blankets sliding off her shoulders. "Lie down," I said to her. "You can't come. I'm wearing your skirt."

Robin was too ill to stand up to me. Normally she has a long, weak persistence, so that I end up losing. But she just lay down and cried.

"Now she's crying!" I said. "She cries like a weapon. Lie down, Robin." I was really horrible. Duck and Hern looked on, subdued. They wanted to see Kankredin too much to interfere. "Let's build her a shelter to keep the rain off," I said to them, "and then go."

The cats got into the shelter gladly. We put food and water in it, and Gull. Nobody argued about Gull. We knew he must stay. Robin was still tearful, but I am almost sure she was glad to be staying, too. We tucked her up where she could see the One's fire before we ran the boat down to the brown racing tide.

Though we put the sail up, it was the tide which took us and snatched us toward the sandbanks at the Rivermouth. It snatched so fiercely that I took up the Young One. I was afraid already. Duck had the Lady in his hands the moment the boat was in the water. Hern smiled scornfully, but he was shaking whenever I looked at him.

It was impossible to see far in the whiteness and grayness of the rain, but I think the River goes into the sea through many channels, among banks of sand and marsh. The place is miles wide, and low and wet. It was lucky Kars Adon had mentioned the tide because the place where our boat went through was shallow enough as it was. Without the race of the water, we would have run aground. We could not see any distance. Our boat drew on swiftly, drawing with it, as it were, the circle of what we could see. At first we saw water; then, on both sides, there was sticky, shiny marsh, sometimes like wet sand, sometimes covered with brown plants. Even in our small circle, there were more birds than I could count. I saw herons wading, River birds swimming and diving, geese, ducks, grebes, coots, and more gulls than I thought possible, glimmering white through the white rain. Everywhere came cries and squawks, splashings, and the beating of wings. And with every yard, our fear grew.

"I bet the fishing's good here," Duck said. His teeth chattered. Yet it felt hot and airless among the beating wings. The rain dewed our rugcoats and filled our hair, and we did not feel cold.

Then we saw something dark through the rain ahead. It was not a ship. We could see the darkness crossed our channel and ran off on either side. Black fear grew in us. We leaned forward, trying to see through the veils of rain. We saw what seemed to be a small boat being poled across in front of the obstruction, just at the limit of what we could see. It went slowly, but we could barely see it all the same. We saw the fair heads of Heathens in it. One was poling, the other stooping and flinging things from the water into the boat. They had gone, slowly to the right, before we could see more.

We knew—though I do not know how—that we had seen something terrible.

"Mother!" whispered Duck. "What were they do-ing?"

"Fishing, I should think," said Hern. But from the way he shivered in the heat and wet, he did not believe it.

"Let's go back!" I said. But the tide was taking us on all the time, and we could not. "Oh," I said, "why is the One in his fire just when we need him most?" We were slipping forward between the banks of croaking, splashing birds, and I still could not see what the black thing was across our way. I hugged the Young One to my chest and prayed to him to help us.

"Mother!" whimpered Duck again.

"Shut up! She's dead," said Hern.

We slid on. The white rain veiled us. Everywhere was white. We slid in a white circle on gray water, and even the marsh was hidden. I heard a duck croak and a gull cry overhead. My fear of gulls made me look up, but I could not see the bird. The rain seemed to have stopped. Not so fearsome, you think? Next moment our boat drifted upon two ducks, which flew off from almost beneath it, with a great outcry. And we could not see the ducks. You know how ducks run through the water, flapping, until at last they have speed enough to fly. We saw the splash and scuffle in two lines on the water, the spray and drips as the wings beat the surface on either side, and we saw the last splash as they rose on the wing. We heard their quacking. We felt the whir of the wings on our faces. But there were no ducks.

"What's happened?" whispered Duck.

"We've not gone blind," said Hern. His voice

cracked. "We can see the water," he said. He was not steering anymore. He was crouched with one arm on the tiller, gazing as if he could force his eyes to see again.

The boat turned sideways and drifted on. I saw the deep V of a swimming grebe, and many scutterings upon the water. I heard birds overhead. But not a single one did I see until, without break or warning, we were out at sea and I could see the birds again.

The obstruction stood behind us. It was a great net, as high as a house, black as midnight and made in large squares. It was hung on posts as far as we could see in both directions, across the marshes and across the many trickling mouths of the River, from one shore to the other. The birds were in the mud behind the net, feeding and flapping as before. We could see them perfectly. In the distance, also behind the net, we saw the boat with the two Heathens in it, still at their strange business.

On the other side of us was wide blueness. The sea is a great field of water. Where it meets the sky, it is a darker blue. It is immense, too big for me. I was glad to fix my eyes on the long black ship moored to lines not far away. It swung on its ropes as I looked. There were two big eyes painted one on either side of its sharp black prow, with which it seemed to stare at us.

"Look, look! In the net!" said Duck.

There were things struggling against the net, on the River side of it. They were not clearly to be seen.

They were large, for the most part, the size of geese or swans, and I think they were winged and of a pinkish color. Each one, as it came against the black net, struggled furiously to get through. We could see the struggle more easily than the thing which fought. Some were able to force themselves through the wide mesh. These flew off to the sea over our heads and were lost in the blue. Many, many more gave up the struggle and slithered down the net inside. The water there was full of their strugglings and floppings. It was these that the Heathens in the boat were collecting.

"People's souls," said Duck.

"I don't believe it!" said Hern, staring. "I don't *believe* it!"

Just then the Heathens in the small boat saw us. They shouted angrily and came poling back along the net. Hern quickly swung the tiller and let the wind to our sail. It was a fine breezy day out there. I think the rain and the mist were made by the net. In the breeze and the tide we raced toward the black ship and came in under one of its great eyes. I wanted to hide. It stared so.

"It's only paint," said Duck as he moored our boat to the great chain that held the black ship to the bottom of the sea. Hern hoisted himself up it, onto the deck. Duck looked at me and put the Lady into his shirt, under his rugcoat. I did the same with the Young One before we followed Hern.

The floor of the ship was black and smelled of tar.

Overhead it was like a winter forest—ropes upon ropes hanging from masts that were trees braced with iron hoops. There was no one to be seen. But a number of large wicker baskets stood along the sides. Duck opened one. He sprang back, and so did Hern and I, when a host of the almost unseen winged things whirled up out of it, with a noise like roaring flames. They did not hurt us. They flew in a stream over the side of the ship and vanished seaward.

Before we had recovered from the shock of that, a door in the high black stern flew open. Heathens dashed out of it, shouting, "Who are you? What do you think you're doing?"

These were mages. I knew it. When Uncle Kestrel first told us of the Heathen enchanters and their battle spells, I had imagined ugly yellow-haired men with large mauve noses, creased cheeks, and crooked mouths. It surprised me that Tanamil and, later, Kars Adon were not like that. But these men were just like my imaginings. It makes me think a man does not become a Heathen mage unless he is too unpleasant to find friends any other way. They wore gowns that trailed, which they had to hold up as they ran shouting toward us. I was very frightened and clutched the Young One under my rugcoat.

I think Hern had learned from Kars Adon. He stood there calmly and bowed to them a little as they rushed toward us. This made them pause. They did not lay hold of us—as they had meant to when they first saw us—but they crowded threateningly round. With all those ugly faces so close, I do not think Hern was as calm as he looked.

"What do you brats want?" they demanded.

"We are mages with a message from Kars Adon," Hern said. "May we speak to Kankredin if you please?"

The ugly faces circled round us, arguing. "These aren't mages." "Yes, they are. They came through the net." "He won't want to be bothered with brats!" "Put a weight spell on them and tip them overboard." I was very confused. While they milled around us, I kept seeing words and scraps of sentences. Each of them had sayings woven in his gown. It seems they had this art, too. They were large words, and boastful. *I tortured the beast in*—I read. *I took the eyes off Sandar*. Then again:—*made jewels where none were in*—and—*three dead in one spell* and *I sent the hidden death*. It was enough to make one ill.

"Silence!" someone boomed at the other end of the ship. "What is this?"

"Three brats saying they're mages, sir," someone called.

"Did they pass through the net?" the voice boomed.

"Yes, sir. Ladri's shouting about it from the soul-boat, sir."

"Then I suppose I'd better see them," roared the voice. "Bring them in."

We were hustled along the deck and through the door at the end. There was a room there with hammocks slung from big beams, but we went straight through that into another room right in the stern. This room had a big window looking on the sea, and one empty chair—a good chair, much better than Kars Adon's. They pushed us in front of it and stood milling behind.

"Some of you get out!" boomed Kankredin. He was sitting in the chair. It was empty till then.

I had thought, after seeing that net of souls, that nothing could frighten me anymore, but I was wrong. Kankredin was not Tanamil. He was not young. He was old—old in the way a stone is old, hard and lasting and as if he had never been otherwise. And like a stone when you turn it over in the earth, a coldness breathed off him. He froze my skin and lifted the hairs on my arms even before I looked at him properly.

It was not easy to look at him. The coldness of him numbed my eyes. I think he had a wriggly gray sheet of hair on either side of his face, and that the top of his head was bald and gray with dirt, with one or two big pink lumps on it. That is what you notice first when a person is sitting down. Then he lifted his face, numbingly, and it seemed to be a plump face, with the eyes thick-lidded, in folds. But as soon as I met his eyes, the face grew and removed itself, to seem large and faint and far away. Hern says he can still see it like that when he closes his eyes, but he cannot tell what he sees. It is the same for me. I remember his voice better, telling the mages to get out. It sounded out of his great chest and belly like the clapper in a bell. But it was a bell in the distance. The voice did not seem to come from Kankredin's mouth. It came clanging from a way off, sounding of fear and horror, defeat and death. As soon as I heard it, I knew we were standing in front of a great evil, and I saw we were mad to have come without the One.

The thing I saw most clearly was the gown Kankredin was swathed in. It was long and voluminous. Unlike the gowns of the other mages, his was woven all over with words, from collar to hem, and the words were much larger and looser than I would weave them. At first I could not look at those words. They leaped from the cloth, close and violent, as if they would do damage to anyone who read them. I had to turn my eyes aside. It was too hard to see Kankredin and too easy to see his gown.

I know Kankredin was not Tanamil. Yet I had, all through, a strong feeling that Tanamil was close by. I looked round for him among the other mages, but these had all left the room by then, except for *I tortured the beast* and *hidden death*.

"Well?" Kankredin clanged out, looking up at us. "You passed through the net without losing your souls, and I daresay you think yourselves mighty clever. What way did you do it?"

It came to me then that we had, most oddly, arrived on the far side of the net, but I could not say how this was. Duck said airily, "I think it may be a spell you don't know."

"There are no spells that I don't know," Kankredin

thundered out of the distance. "Have you any means of stopping me taking your soul now you're here? Eh?"

"I don't know until you try," Duck said.

"Then we shall see," said Kankredin. "I see you fancy yourself as a mage, boy. Not much of a one, by the looks of it. What's that spell on the edge of that extraordinary native garment you're wearing?"

Duck lifted the sleeve of his rugcoat. Hern's and mine are plain, but Duck, because he was the youngest, has bands at the wrist, very faded now, which say *Duck* many times, in all the duck colors. Duck was annoyed to have such a babyish thing noticed. "Just my name," he said crossly.

"Pretty poor stuff, eh?" said Kankredin. "And a silly name. And you, girl—turn round and let me see it— what on earth is *that* on your skirt? Eh?"

I was very much ashamed, and angry, too. That skirt of Robin's is my worst piece of weaving ever. It says *A man came over the hill* muddle muddle *lady in the mill* muddle muddle. Then it takes a step down and goes, muddle *from the river* muddle *lived forever*. Terrible. In two broad bands round the bottom. The ugly mages both sniggered as they read it, and Kankredin chuckled. His laughter was as bad as his voice. It had such echoes of cruelty that it made me think someone was being tortured behind his chair.

"What kind of spell do you call that?" he boomed.

"It's a nursery rhyme!" I said angrily.

"In baby talk," said Kankredin. He turned, laughing

and torturing, to Hern. "At least you have the sense to go plain," he said.

"I have a message for you," said Hern. It was an odd thing. Duck and I were never as troubled by Kankredin as Hern was. He was pale from the beginning, and before long, he was sweating and breathing heavily. Duck and I each had our Undying, of course, but I think Hern's trouble was more than that. Hern still thought he could fight Kankredin with reason. Reason was overthrown when we saw the souls struggle in the net, but Hern would not admit it. "I've come from Kars Adon—" he began.

"What does that stupid boy want now? Eh?" said Kankredin. He had a terrible way of saying "Eh?" It dragged at you for an answer and bullied you even if you meant to answer. If you resolved to say nothing, you still found you were replying to that "Eh?"

"I am to tell you," Hern said, as if he were struggling, "that Kars Adon is going inland today. He says—"

"He can go, and be eaten by the natives, then," said Kankredin. "I can't be bothered with him. If he had stayed, I'd have let him share my victory, but as it is, I'll make do with the natives. Was that all? Eh?"

"No," said Hern, struggling still. "I want to know what you think you're doing to the River."

"What impertinence is this?" Kankredin boomed, rising to his feet. "Eh?" The cold that came off him made us step back.

Now I must explain that I do not remember well what was said after this point because it was then that I started to read Kankredin's gown. I have to rely on Duck's memory, which is good, but not as good as mine. Hern confesses that from then on his mind felt as if he had his head underwater. His ears were roaring. He remembers little except a struggle with Kankredin to keep his soul.

My reading started first, idly, as Kankredin stood up. As I stepped back, I saw at his left shoulder *I, Kankredin, mage of mages, have set these spells to conquer and confound this land.* It was just level with my eyes. After that, I had to read on. *First I studied deeply,* I read, *to find where the soul and substance of the land lay, for there only may a land be truly conquered. And soon I came to conclude that the soul of the land lies in the one mighty river, which, with his tributary, waters all the country. This river*—this is correct, for he used all through the common weaving for *river,* not the one Tanamil taught me—*this river lies at his source, coiled, I conceive, like a snake or a dragon. Him I catch with this net of words, between sleeping and waking, and bind him fast. But his strength is not yet*—

Here Kankredin sat down, and the next lines were lost in the fold between his belly and his legs. I had to move on to his left thigh.

Meanwhile, Duck tells me, Kankredin was abusing Hern for daring to ask what he was doing to the River. "I am working night and day with the River, bringing his waters down to drown the natives, cleansing the land for us, and you have the gall to stand there asking what I *think* I'm doing!"

Duck answered, seeing Hern struggling and panting, that it was generally thought the River was angry.

"Angry? Of course he's angry!" Kankredin thundered. "He's fighting me tooth and nail. But I'm winning. I have him in a stranglehold, and he won't escape." Duck says Kankredin roared on in this way for some time. Duck listened scornfully because he was sure Kankredin had no idea of the truth about the River. This was just how I felt, reading Kankredin's gown, though Kankredin was saying one thing to Duck and another on his gown.

—*come to my terms*, was the next thing I read. *Thus I keep him tame and pull from him the vital strength of the land. But he has been cunning and fixed his strength in certain of the souls of his people. When I knew this, I sent forth my mages to battle to seek these souls.*

The weaving was large and loose. The next part was on Kankredin's right shoulder. *Then I put my first command on this river that he yield up to me these souls, which he was not willing to do. We strive, and he turns rotten with the effort, bringing sickness, for which I curse him*—Kankredin had pulled the gown up into folds here, at the top of his right leg. I stared and stared, but I could only pick out disjointed fragments at the surfaces of the folds—*refuses the land his waters . . . hides his souls from me . . . send forth greater strength . . . by this I invoke total power*—

"Why do you think I put up the soulnet?" Kankredin roared, as Duck tells me.

"To catch the natives' souls, I suppose," Duck said. "Did you know that quite a lot of the souls were getting through?"

This made Kankredin very annoyed, though he tried not to show it. "So you have mage sight," he said scornfully. "Quite a lot of people can see souls without being mages. Are you telling me to use a smaller mesh? Eh?"

"You'd catch more if you did," said Duck. "What do you do with them?"

"Never you mind," said Kankredin. "That net is a charm on the River, not a soul trap in any strict sense."

"I see," said Duck. Not that he did, he says. But he was enjoying himself, I could tell. I remember thinking, as I stared at Kankredin's gown, that I had seldom seen Duck more confident.

Then, pulled up on to Kankredin's thigh, I read: *and thus we took one with such a soul, outwitting the river by accident, I confess, since his captors had thought he was a clansman like themselves.* I knew he was talking about Gull. I read furiously. *The river would not yield me the soul of the lad, though we strove for three days. But I am cunning. I examined the lad and turned his soul about in my mind. I find his soul is more than the river. It is part of the ancient life behind the river.*

Here came the hem, drawn up above Kankredin's fat vague foot in a dirty sandal. The rest was on the back of the gown. I could have screamed.

I had to get Kankredin to stand up and turn round.
I have never been so determined about anything. I
looked at Duck and turned my hand round inside my
sleeve, hoping that Kankredin would not notice. Duck
understood. He had been trying to read Kankredin's
gown, too, but he is slower than me, and he could see
I was devouring it. So he gave me his daft look, which
is his private way of saying, Yes, but it's not easy, and
turned to Kankredin's two mages.

"Do you do illusions? Can you make yourselves look
like somebody else?" I knew he was trying to find out
if any of them had been disguised as Tanamil, and I
wondered if I dared to shake my head at him. I was
sure the back of Kankredin's robe would tell me.

Kankredin and his two mages gave out sounds of
disgust. But this is exactly what they would do if they
did not want us to know. Duck did not see it that way.

"Yes, but can you?" he said. "Can you stand up and
show me?"

Kankredin saw there was some trick in this. He was
terrifying clever. For a moment the fat shape of his
face became near and clear to see. His thick lids folded
down over his eyes, and he stared at Duck. Duck, for
the first time, was troubled by his power. The front
of his coat heaved as he grasped the Lady, and he
gasped. "That'll teach you to bother me with silly
questions," said Kankredin. "Won't it? Eh?"

At this, I thought suddenly: Why is he bothering
to talk to us at all? He thinks we're just silly children.

I looked at Hern, and Hern was beginning to look the way Gull had looked.

"Stop it!" I said. "Leave my brother's soul alone!"

"Not I," said Kankredin. "There's some strangeness in this soul." He looked full at Hern. Hern put his hands to his face as if he felt giddy.

Duck and I were both terrified. Duck took Hern's arm and pulled him away across the room. And Kankredin sprang out of his chair in a wave of cold air, roaring that Duck was not to meddle.

The next part was very horrible. I had a perfect opportunity to read Kankredin's back, but it was at Hern's expense. And it came to me then that if Kankredin's gown told the truth—and I think it did, as far as Kankredin knew the truth—Hern's soul, and mine, and Duck's were all like Gull's and could be used the same way. Kankredin stared under his fat lids at Hern, and Hern leaned against Duck, shaking. Duck put both arms round Hern and pressed the Lady against him so that they both had a bruise for days. At the same time, he says, he was willing Hern's soul with all his might to look normal—like Korib the miller's son's, like Aunt Zara's, even like Zwitt's. And I read Kankredin's broad back for dear life.

Thus I, Kankredin, mage of mages, know how to rule the very soul of this land's soul. The river tries to keep the lad's soul from me, but I have bound the lad to come to me. I feel him approaching. He is near. By the power of these words and the hands of my mages, I now erect a soulnet across the mouths of the river wherein shall lodge the souls of all those dead in the land. These my mages collect daily. They shall be captive to me and learn to do my bidding, and I shall not suffer them to go out over the sea to their last home. But the lad who is coming to me will lodge in the net in his own body. Then through him I shall draw forth the soul behind the river's soul. When I have it, I shall come up the river, rolling it before me like a wave of the sea, and the land will lie captive at my feet. I, Kankredin, have spoken.

I did not read his sleeves. They seemed to be spells from much longer ago. "Duck! Let's go!" I shrieked.

Kankredin turned and looked under his fat lids at me. I did not think we would be able to go.

"There's no mystery about us," I said. "We—we have to catch up with Kars Adon."

"That's right," Duck said quickly. "Take a look at our souls. Can't you see we're quite open and honest?"

"I've looked at your souls," said Kankredin. "Empty things they are. Suspiciously empty. His is not." He pointed to Hern.

"He's older than us," I said. "And I admit you're doing quite right to wrestle with the River. I think you're very clever. I think—" I would have said anything, anything.

Kankredin laughed at me, with his cruel chuckle, and looked at his two mages. "What shall we do?"

"They're absolute idiots," *hidden death* said, but he said it with a sour kind of slyness, meaning something else.

"Exactly," said Kankredin, agreeing to this something else. "All right," he said to us. "If you can get back through the net again, you're free to go. Go and try. I shall enjoy watching you."

I do not remember going out through the room with the hammocks. I think Kankredin hurled us out on deck, where Hern staggered about.

"You get the boat cast off," I said to Duck. "I'll bring Hern." I thought it would be like Gull all over again.

But Hern is tougher than Gull. As Duck raced down the black decking, Hern pushed me away and dived at the baskets ranged against the side. "You do the other side!" he shouted. He went staggering up the whole row, throwing up the lids. I am still amazed at Hern thinking of the trapped souls. But he must have known what they felt like. I threw back wicker lids on the other side of the ship. The roaring wings of the escaping souls mixed with the angry yells of the mages.

Kankredin's voice boomed through it all. "Let them be. We shall take vengeance for that."

The mages left us alone and stood watching as we went down into our boat. I took the tiller. We moved away from the staring eyes of the ship, before all the staring faces of the mages lining the side of it, and two more sitting staring in the soulboat nearby. We felt the jeers in the staring, but there seemed nothing we could do except sail for the net.

I was too shaken to manage the boat well, and the tide was against us. Duck took out an oar to help, but we still drifted crankily sideways. We could see mouth after mouth of the River passing behind the great black net, until the black ship looked small behind us. Then at last we drifted up against the net. A soul or two struggled in it above our heads, and we were just the same, going the opposite way.

Kankredin's voice boomed across the water. "Go on! Go through the net!" We knew he was playing cat and mouse with us.

"He'll fetch us back in a minute," said Hern. "We can't get through."

"We can try this," said Duck. He put the oar away and carefully took out of his shirt the pipes Tanamil had made for him. He saw the way I looked at him. He said, "I'm almost sure Tanamil isn't one of them. And it's worth a try even if it's using their own enchantment against them. Keep us going for the net."

Duck put the pipes to his mouth and played. His music was nothing like Tanamil's. It was bold and jerky and full of breath. But he had scarcely played half a tune when I looked up at the net and found its blackness misted over, with mist beyond.

Kankredin's voice boomed out. "Duck! Stop that silly piping. Stop it!"

Duck faltered and lost the tune. The net swung before me, black and clear. "Go on," I said. "It works!"

"I can't," said Duck. "Not with him shouting at me."

"Duck! Come here to me!" Kankredin boomed.

Hern looked up. "He's not shouting at you. Your name's Mallard. Keep playing, and don't be a fool. He's worried stiff we're getting away." Hern was right. The two mages in the soulboat were poling toward us as fast as they could go.

Duck played again, fierce and squeaky with haste. His face was red with it. The net turned from black to gray, and then it was not there. We were moving forward in whiteness. In a moment, as before, there were birds all round us that we could not see. This time we were heartily glad of it. Duck played and played us forward into whiteness, until at last he had to leave off and lean over, panting. By then the net was behind us some way and the wide sands of the Rivermouth in front.

"You did it!" I said. "How did you know?"

Duck wiped the pipes and put them carefully away. "Everything goes away like that quite often when I play," he said. "I thought I was out of breath the first time. You know, I think I shall be a magician when I grow up. I shall be a better one than Kankredin."

"Hey! Tanaqui! Look where you're sailing!" said Hern.

He was a little late saying it. I was looking at Duck. We ran deep aground in a reed flat with our keel down, and we stuck. This was how we came to be captured by our own people. Maybe it was Kankredin's malice. I am sure it was my fault for leaving the One in his fire.

* * *

I am now at the back hem of my rugcoat. All I have space to say is that we are at a stand. Gull is still a clay figure. Robin is ill. I am afraid she will die. I sit with her in the old mill across from Shelling, with no help from my gloomy brothers. Even if Robin were well enough for us to run away, Zwitt would have us killed if he found us on our own. It is a bad thing to wish to run away from our own King, but I wish I could. Instead all I can do is weave and hope for understanding. The meaning of our journey is now in this rugcoat. I am Tanaqui, and I end my weaving.

:❙ PART TWO ❙:

The Second Coat

:|| 1 ||:

I AM TANAQUI. I must begin on a second rugcoat because understanding has come to me at last, and maybe I no longer need to blame myself.

My dream of my mother came to me again the night I finished the first coat. It troubled me. Why should my mother tell me to think? What should I think about except that I have wronged the One twice now? I started the first coat because of this dream, but when the dream came again, I began to suspect that my weaving was not enough. I am glad Uncle Kestrel brought me all my yarn, even that which was under the broken part of the roof. I still feel bitter about that. Zwitt need not have broken our house. But the wool has dried out now, and I think there is enough of every color to make another coat.

I will tell first how I wronged the One again. We were caught while we stuck on the mudbank because we had still not grasped the nature of the mud there. Hern jumped overboard to push us off and sank in it beyond his knees. He was so weak after our meeting with Kankredin that he could hardly struggle back into the boat, and he was very angry with me. I told him that it was because I had made them leave the One in his fire.

"Don't talk such nonsense!" Hern said. "It doesn't mean you have to steer straight into a mudbank."

We tried rocking the boat to loose it. The water trickled from the mud continually and held the keel fast. We should have seen from that that the mud was getting firmer, but we did not. We were too taken up with looking anxiously at the mist where the soulnet stood, thinking Kankredin was bound to follow us. No mages came. I think Kankredin had decided we were not worth the trouble. But we were taken completely by surprise when men of our own people came running over the mud from behind us and dragged us out of the boat, thinking we were Heathens.

We screamed that we were not Heathens, but they did not believe us and dragged us away a full mile over the mud and sand. All the while, they were saying things like "I look forward to hearing these squeal" and "I'm going to take it out on these for Litha. I'll make it long and sweet." I think we were all crying by the time they pushed us over the sand dune and into a camp of some size. We were desperate by then that they should know we were not Heathens.

Someone who saw us being brought in said, "You had a bit of luck, didn't you? I'll put you all down for a reward. Bring them along, and let's see what we can make of them."

They pushed us into a clear space where a great tree lay, dead and silver. The man who had spoken sat on this tree, and many others—the way our people do—came crowding from the tents to look. I heard someone call, "Come on, Jay! Heathens for lunch!"

The man who had hold of me—his name is Sard and I still do not like him—shook me and said, "Now you behave. This is the King. King, understand? He eats you Heathen for breakfast, he does."

I could hardly credit it, but it was indeed our King. I was nearly too awed to look at him. This was not, like Kars Adon, a boy and a Heathen. This was a true King. I took a quick look from under my hair. I saw a small plump man of about middle age. At one time, I think, he has been quite stout, but he lost flesh in the wars, they say. His face is still chubby, however, with a pout to the lips and a humorous twist to it. There were bags under his eyes, and his eyes looked bright and dark, twinkling upon the bags.

"Where were they?" our King said to Sard.

"Run aground on Carne Bank, Majesty," Sard replied, grinning. "I thought even Heathens had more sense."

Our King looked at us. "Where are you from? Where is your clan and how many are you?"

Hern stood with his head down, glowering at our King. "We're not Heathens," he said. Then Duck and I began to clamor at our King, trying to convince him we were not Heathens in every way we knew.

Our King leaned back and folded his arms, sighing. As we talked, I heard him say humorously to the man who stood behind him, "Why do they all make this fuss, Jay?" It was so clear he was not listening that I stopped talking in despair. Hern and Duck had stopped already. "Finished?" asked our King, twinkling his eyes at us. "Right. Now I don't like using unpleasant methods with youngsters, but I assure you I shall if you won't talk. I want to know where your camp is. Who's your chief, or earl, or whatever you call it? How many Heathen are you? Not that it will help much, as you seem to swarm like vermin, but still—we do what we can. Now tell me, and I may spare your lives."

"Majesty, we were truly born in Shelling, up the River," I said. Our King smiled. I cast about for a face that might believe me. All smiled. The man called Jay, who stood behind the King, smiled broadest of all. I knew him. He had only one arm now and his red rugcoat was gray and ragged, but he had smiled like that at Robin, when she stood with her arms all floury. "You came to Shelling," I said. "You took my father and my brother Gull to the wars. Don't you remember?"

"You saw me there," said Hern. "You said I was too young."

"I went to a lot of places," the man Jay said, smiling still.

"And you smiled at my sister," said Duck.

Jay looked at me and choked. "She's a bit young for me."

"Not that one, stupid! The other one," said Hern.

"I do smile at girls," Jay said, grinning widely. "I've even been known to wink at Heathens. They picked this up, Majesty," he said to our King, "from some poor soul they tormented."

"They must have done," our King agreed.

At that I became so frantic that I could think of only one way to convince the King I was no Heathen. "Look," I said, "I'll prove we're not Heathens. Here is one of our Undying." I dragged the Young One from the front of my shirt and held him toward the King.

Our King twinkled at me. "So you're a thief, too?"

"No, no!" I said. "Heathens don't have Undying. We have the Lady as well as the Young One." Duck scowled at me and shook his head, but I went on. "The greatest of our Undying is the One. I can't show him to you because he's in his fire at the moment—he always has to go in his fire when the floods go down— but please believe me!"

"A nice story," said the man Jay.

But our King leaned forward, with a twinkle of interest in his eyes and only the barest smile on his face. I have never known him quite without a smile. "This One of yours," he said. "What color is he?"

Hern and Duck both glared at me, but I said, as if I could not stop, "Dark, with glistering specks, but—"

"Shut up, Tanaqui!" said Duck.

"—but he changes each time he goes in his fire," I said.

Our King gestured to Duck that he was to hold his tongue. Then he leaned to me further, and said, "Name me his secret names."

"They're secret," I said. By this time I was horrified, but it was like the rapids at the end of the lake. I had gone too far to stop.

"Come here and name them in my ear," said our King.

I am ashamed when I weave this, but I did so. I went up to our King—he smelled of sweat and horse and, just a little, of cloves—and I whispered, "He is called Adon and Amil and Oreth." That is how I wronged the One. But I went on and wronged him further because when the King asked me, I told him the One's fire was on our island and that Robin was there, unwell, too. And I described which our island was, in spite of the way Hern and Duck looked at me.

Our King sat back and puckered his face toward Jay and the others nearest him. "Well, what do you think?"

"There's quite a nest of Heathen over there," one of them said. "It looks like the perfect trap to me."

"I know," our King agreed. "But let's say curiosity

killed the King. Or that somebody slipped up in Shelling last autumn. Jay— Oh, I forgot. Can you manage one-handed?"

"Provided the remaining hand's tied behind my back" was Jay's reply.

"Good," said the King. "Tie your hand up, take ten men and the best boat—and the elder boy, I think—and let him show you the place. Bring back anything you find there."

"I'm glad you said me," Hern said. He spoke very rudely because he was angry with me. "I'd have had to ask you to send me if you hadn't. I'm head of the family, and it has to be me who takes the One out of the fire."

"Oddly enough, I thought of that," our King said to him. "And I thought the other two could stay as hostages for your good faith. Move, Jay!"

My punishment was that I never saw the One taken out of the fire. The King's camp was right on the other side of the Rivermouth from our island. Duck and I had to wait two hours for Jay to cross and come back. We sat on a sandbank watching the King's men bustling in the camp. Their tents are good, in many color, but the people are few—not more than fifty, all men. It ought to have seemed more warlike than the poor huts of Kars Adon, because there were no women, no rubbish heaps, and no children but Duck and me, but it did not, and never does. It is more as if our King were traveling for a holiday.

While we waited, Duck was so angry with me that he only spoke once. "Did Kankredin's coat say how we can get Gull back?" he said.

"No," I said. "It said Gull was coming to him. The net is to catch Gull, and he's waiting for him before he conquers the country. And it can't be wrong to tell our own King about the One."

"If he thinks Gull's still on his way," Duck said, "then I was right, and Tanamil isn't one of his mages. And you know we're not supposed to talk about the One to anybody." And he said nothing else.

At last there was a great shout that the boat was coming. Everyone, our King included, went running through the hills of sand to the shore. We ran with them. We were part of the crowd jostling on the shingle, and we helped to pull the boat out of the falling waves. It was large and high. Jay appeared head and shoulders above the gunwale.

"Well?" said the King.

"Everything as described," said Jay. "This is the list—start unloading. Three cats." Sweetheart, Rusty, and Ratchet were dropped down beside our King. They were ruffled and not pleased. Our King looked at them in amusement. "Ten blankets," said Jay, and these were dropped on the shore, too. "Two sacks, containing cheese, dried fish, and onions mostly." The sacks followed our blankets. "And," said Jay, "one sick young lady."

I thought they were going to drop Robin on the shore, too. In fact, they lowered her very carefully, and Hern climbed down to make sure she was safe. They had wrapped her in Jay's rugcoat. She was worse again. She says it was the shock of Jay's coming, on top of worry about us. I put a blanket round her as she shivered on the pebbles, and she cried because Duck and I were still alive.

"And?" said our King, holding out his hand to Jay. "Nothing else?"

"With her," Jay said, nodding down at Robin.

It seemed that Hern had no sooner taken the One from his fire than he gave him into Robin's hands. Robin would let nobody near him. I could not think why Hern had done this, until Hern said, "Come and see," and beckoned Duck over, too.

Robin unwrapped her hand from the great folds of Jay's rugcoat and showed us the One clasped in it. He was gold. He shone all over with a mild orange luster and seemed to be made of metal. Hern and Robin could understand it no more than we could. Hern said he had found the One shining even more brightly in the ashes of the fire. He had dulled a little in the air since. And, Hern says, there was such naked greed on the faces of Jay and the others that he gave the One to Robin, instinctively as it were, to keep him safe. How he thinks poor Robin would be able to keep the One if somebody twisted her wrist, I do not know. She has Gull to keep, too, wrapped in her own rugcoat, and no one knows of him but us four.

Up to this moment Robin has most valiantly fulfilled Hern's trust. She wrapped the One away when the

King came up and refused to let him be seen. A faint pink came into her pale face at having to treat our King so, but she was firm.

"He is not to be bandied about and looked at by everyone," she said.

"If you all came into my tent and looked at him over supper?" our King suggested. "I could set up a hearth to make him feel more at home."

Our King was being very polite now, but Robin looked at him severely. She is not used to people making jests all the time, the way our King does. But she agreed.

Our King insisted on a polite and lavish supper. It was a trial to Duck and me, though not to Hern. Hern likes eating and does not care about manners. It was a trial to Robin, too, because she was not really well enough, but I was glad she was there. People believe Robin. When she said we were not Heathens, our King assured her it had been an unfortunate mistake.

"May I see the One now?" he asked when we had eaten fish and meat. There was a pause then, before they brought in chickens, eggs, and sweetmeats. No wonder our King is chubby.

Robin reluctantly brought out the One and stood him on the table among the King's fine dishes. He was the finest thing there. Our King put out a hand to him, looked quizzically at Robin, and at last picked him up. We could see the One was heavy. Robin says he weighs twice what he did.

"Solid gold!" said our King. "I swear to it! This is his

latest change, is it?" We nodded. Our King carefully turned the One around to have his face beneath the lamp. Now that he is gold, the One's features are much easier to see. He has a strong nose, a little like Hern's or Gull's. The King saw this. I saw him look at Hern's profile. "How long has this fellow been in your family?" he asked Robin.

"For as long as anyone knows, my father told me, Majesty," Robin replied.

"Hmm," said our King. "Your family must once have been a very important one, young lady, did you know that? And you truly put him in a fire every year after the floods?"

"Every year," said Robin. "My father said we have never once missed."

"That was the sign by which I knew him," our King said, turning the One over. "You have been faithful to the bargain your ancestors made with him. Do you know who he is, this golden gentleman?" He waved the One toward us, from side to side, not wholly respectfully.

"Yes," I said. "He's the One."

"That's a silly sort of name," said our King. "You told me his real names earlier. My fluffy-haired maiden, he is the River—the great River himself! What do you think of that?"

"I think it isn't true," I said.

"Oh, yes, it is true," said he, still waving the One about. "We Kings have a hard time of it and have to put up with a great deal from our subjects—flat

contradictions from little girls, among other things—
but our reward is that we are told more than most
people. I know about your One. As a matter of fact,
I had him searched for when the Heathen came. If
only Jay had found him when he came to Shelling, I
wouldn't be in this pickle now. He could have got us
out of it. Only fancy him turning up like this! You'd
almost think he did it on purpose. What do you think
you're playing at, you stupid golden beggar?" he said
to the One. "It wasn't nice to hide away!" This was
not quite a joke—or only a joke in the way that everything our King says is a sort of joke. I could see Robin
was shocked.

"How do you know he's the River?" Hern asked
bluntly. I could say that Hern was tired out after our
day's troubles, and it would be true. On the other
hand, I have never once heard him speak respectfully
to our King.

"Knowledge is handed down from King to King,"
said our King. "When our people first came to this
land, there was a Queen called Cenblith, who may
have been a many-greats-grandmother of yours as well
as mine, I think. She found a way to bind the River
to the service of man. They say she was a witch. I
think it just as possible she was simply very pretty,
and the River fell for her like a waterfall. Anyway, he
submitted to be bound. He agreed among other things
to support our people in battle with his not inconsider-
able strength, which strength he obligingly let Cen-

blith put into this small image of himself. But he made one condition: that he be put into a fire once a year. When his dross was purged and he turned to gold, then he would be at his utmost power. And here he is, golden and too late!" The King's eyes twinkled almost as if they were wet, as he looked at the One between his hands.

I remember looking at the One and wondering about the great floods and Kankredin's struggle with the River. I still do not believe the One and the River are the same—or not quite the same.

"He was daft to let himself be bound," Duck said.

"I agree, but I am very glad he did," said our King. He held the One up toward the colored roof of the tent. "Now we can prosper and succeed together," he said. "Now I've got you, you slippery golden beggar!"

"Majesty," said Robin, "the One is ours."

"So he is, young lady," said our King. "You shall stay with me and keep him for me." He passed the One to Robin. "There. Back to his rightful guardians. Keep him safe. We have a lot of traveling before us, now the floods are down."

And travel we did that next morning. This is what has made Robin so ill. She has been hurried here and bumped there and made to sit in the rain until the King is ready. After the first day's travel our King had his physician see her. He said it was the River fever and, as she had had it once, she would soon be well and was quite fit to travel. It is this same physician who took off Jay's arm. Jay says if it were not for that physician, he would still have two arms. I share Jay's opinion. Robin does *not* get well, even resting.

The King has taken a fancy to Hern. He gave him a pony to ride, while the rest of us bumped and creaked in the baggage carts. Every evening, I had to attend to Hern's saddle sores, before I could see to Robin. Now I know why Robin so often exclaimed "Why does nobody help me!" Everything falls on me. For the rest of the day the King has Hern beside him. "Fetching and carrying," Hern calls it. He is not in the least grateful. The trouble is, our King loves people who are rude and familiar with him. This is why he is so fond of Jay. So the crosser Hern is, the more the King admires him.

Hern is in a black mood. He does not show half of it to our King. He says he went down the River to rescue Gull or avenge him. He did not believe in enchantments. Yet first Tanamil and then Kankredin defeated him with spells. He could do less than Duck or I could. He was forced to admit that enchantments exist. This has damaged his respect for his own mind.

"But enchantments are of the mind, too," I said.

"Not of *my* mind," said Hern. "That's why I'm a failure. I wasn't even sure people had souls. Then I saw the souls in the net and knew I was looking failure in the face. It's an awful feeling." Yet that was not the whole story, as I found out later.

Duck is gloomy, too, because he is bored.

All this while our King hastened with us across the

country. He does not stay near houses or in any one place for long, for fear of the Heathens. Whenever we come to a farm or a village, the King's men knock at doors and run into houses shouting that the King has come. If the place is empty because of the floods or the Heathens, they take what they can find. When there are people, the King orders what he needs. The people often protest; I know how we should feel if they came banging at our door and carried off all we had saved from winter before the supplies had grown again. The King promises payment and takes so much that we sit high up in the carts on piles of corn and dead sheep. Collet is our King's memory man, and he memorizes the debt. He tells me that he holds many thousand payments in his head, for food or promised rewards. He does not think they will ever be paid.

It was very rough traveling after the floods. Robin suffered more and more because after a while she became too weak to get out and walk in the worst places. "I can't *stand* this anymore!" she said one evening when the sun was down, but we still went jolting on.

Hern had looked in on us, and he saw how ill Robin was. He went and asked the King if we could stop.

"Oh, the light's good for miles more yet," said our King. "Besides, there seem to be Heathens coming up behind." Our King gets news of Heathens from everyone we encounter. And we went on.

I was so angry that I jumped down from the cart and ran among the horses to the King. "Majesty," I shouted. "The One wants us to stop here!"

I did not think the King would listen, but he did. We stopped at once. After that I chose our camping place every day, speaking for the One. We spared Robin a good deal of jolting like that. It amazes me that our King believes I know the One's wishes, but I think it is the one thing he takes seriously. I have become spokesman for the One. Every day the King asks me jestingly, "And what has the golden gentleman to say to me today, fluffyhead?" I could tell him anything.

"If he believes you, he'd believe anything!" Hern said scornfully.

Our King, of course, talks to everyone, freely and cheerfully, but he talked to me much more after that. I cannot be familiar with him. The weight of kingship and all our Kings before him makes him a heavy matter to me. Our position oppresses me, too. We cannot be called prisoners, yet what else are we? So when he makes his jokes, I do not laugh.

"Fluffyhead, you do come of a serious-minded family," he said to me one day, in a brown field, where the grass lay plastered down with mud in long ripples. "Can't you laugh? I know you've had your troubles, but look at me. I've lost my two sons, my wife, and my kingdom, and I can still laugh."

"I expect you're looking forward to conquering the Heathen and getting your kingdom back, Majesty," I said, "and I'm not."

"Great One!" he said, twinkling his eyes at me. "Do

you think so, solemn face? I gave up that idea months ago. The most I hope for is to save my skin until I can get a new heir. It will be my son who benefits from the One's help, not me."

I thought this was just his joke at the time, but it has now become clear to me that our King has indeed no intention of fighting the Heathen again. He inquires daily about the Heathen, but this is in order to avoid them.

Many times it has been on the tip of my tongue to tell him that the Heathen he is running from is only Kars Adon—though I think there are other little bands, too, as Kars Adon said—and that the real menace is Kankredin. But I have not said. Kars Adon is a Heathen and an enemy, but his way is better than our King's. I do not blame our King. Jay has told me how terrible the wars were. But I will not tell him about Kars Adon. Duck will not tell him either. He says our King bores him, and nobody can do anything about Kankredin. As for Hern—well, I found out when we had news of Kars Adon at last.

Summer drew on us as we traveled. We approached the River again, which seemed to revive Robin, and came into the hills at the end of the great lake. The lake was beautiful. It was blue as solid sky. The many trees around it were reflected upside down in the blue. But it was spoiled for me by the people there. They said we were Heathens and stoned us. Duck has a scar from it which will last all his life.

Jay stopped the stoning by saying we were Heathen princes under the protection of the mages. Robin was very angry with Jay.

"What should I have said, lady?" Jay asked. "You try telling them the truth."

While we were there, some men came over the broken bridge, very pleased with themselves. They had fought Kars Adon. They knew it was him by the flags. Kars Adon's people had been surrounded in a valley across the River. Numbers of them were killed before they could fight free.

"Why didn't you kill them all?" our King asked pleasantly.

Hern told me this with a pale face. "The *fool*!" he said. "The stupid fool! Fancy getting himself penned in on low ground!"

Now I know the other part of Hern's misery. As Hern has failed in what he set himself to do, he has taken comfort in the dreams of Kars Adon. He knows it is wrong—that is why he is so moody—but he cannot help himself. I had often wondered why Hern listened so eagerly to the King's daily messages about the Heathen.

He was hoping for news of Kars Adon. Now we have it, it is bad news. Poor Hern. It is lucky our King does not intend to fight the Heathen. Hern would be on both sides at once.

:∥ 2 ∥:

WE JOURNEYED THROUGH forest beyond the lake.
Robin was bounced over tree roots and thrown out of
the cart once. It seemed to me that much more of it
would kill her.

"Go and tell the King the One wants us to stop until
Robin's well," said Duck.

It was an excellent idea. "Suppose I tell him the One
wants us to be left behind in an empty cottage, on our
own?" I said.

"He won't do that," said Duck. "He wants the One."
He was right.

Our King readily agreed to camp until Robin was
well. "Still looking very peaky, isn't she?" he said. He
pointed through the budding green. "Suppose she rests
up in that old mill over there. We'll camp outside, and

the village over the River can send us food. We'll give her a week or so. There don't seem to be any Heathen in these parts."

I had no idea we were near the River. It was all forest to me. Imagine my surprise when I found it was the mill across the River from Shelling—the one that is haunted by a woman, that they say the River forbade them to use. I told the King it would do perfectly. I hoped I would see Zwitt's face when he knew.

Jay went over to Shelling in the punt Uncle Kestrel keeps on the millpond and gave them the King's orders. Shortly Zwitt and some other people came over in boats, bringing a few things and protesting about the rest. I think food was short. The floods had been in all the gardens. But Zwitt would protest if he was sitting on a heap of vegetables a mile high and someone asked him for a carrot.

Zwitt saw Hern with the King and knew him at once. He asked to speak to the King alone. I looked out from the mill and saw them walking together among the forget-me-nots by the millrace. Zwitt, by his face, was uttering dire warnings. Our King was laughing and patting Zwitt on the back. I see why our King was so pleased. Now he knows that we told the truth and the One is indeed the One. I think he came to Shelling on purpose. It is what I would have done in his place, I suppose, but my heart is heavy. He will never let us go now. Hern says Zwitt made the King promise him twice as much as usual, as a fee for leaving us alone. But promises are easy.

"Your friends across the water tell me you put bad spells on them," Jay said to me. "Are you a witch?"

"I wish I was. I'd—I'd turn their feet back to front!" I said.

"Temper, temper, now!" said Jay.

I am still very bitter. From upstairs in the mill, where I sleep, I can see the ruins of our house. Zwitt did that. It was to soothe my bitterness and my worry about Robin that I began to long to weave. Then came my dream. Then Uncle Kestrel.

We made Robin a bed in the dry room on the ground floor. It has a door, for loading flour, which opens onto the River, and I have this open in the daytime so that Robin can see the River. All the time I have been weaving it was at its most beautiful. The water is a deep, shining green, like an eye in the light. It flows lazily, slowly. The sun slants down in beams and turns the water green-gold. Midges circle in. Every so often a fish leaps, or a willow bud falls heavily and swims to the doorstep. But Robin does not enjoy it. And I find it so hard to be patient with her.

That first day I was near shaking her. As we were settled, I wanted Gull with us, where I could see him. If we exchanged him for the Young One, no one but us would know the difference. Robin unwrapped Gull and let me have him. But she would not have the Young One in exchange.

"I won't have him near me," she whined. "Take him away."

I have had to hide the Young One in my bed upstairs. If I even speak of him, Robin begins to cry. And yet she clings to the One so that even I hardly get a glimpse of him. The King came in that evening—as he comes every evening—to inquire after his "golden gentleman." Robin would not let our King look at the One at all.

"I wish the King would leave us alone," she said.

Then Sweetheart put a mouse on her bed, and you would have thought it was a poisonous snake. Then Jay came in. Jay made a lot of noise and merriment. He says laughter cures. But the reason he came, I saw of a sudden, is that he is courting Robin. I was shocked. It does not seem right when Robin is ill. Jay is quite old and has loved many women. He boasts of it. That shocked me, too. But I like Jay all the same. My head was in a muddle about it.

"Do you like Jay enough to marry him?" I asked Robin when Jay had gone.

Robin shuddered. "No! I can't bear the way the stump of his arm wags about!"

It is true. Jay's stump of arm seems to have a life of its own. I do not like to look at it either. "Don't you like him at all?" I said. "He likes you."

"Don't talk about it! I don't want him! I shan't ever marry!" Robin said frantically. I could have kicked myself. It was gone midnight before she was calm enough to go to sleep.

When she did, I opened the door to the River and sat thinking. It seemed to be all my fault, this, because I had twice wronged the One. As I sat, I thought I saw a light in the River. I knelt in the doorway and stared, terrified, down into the green-gold depths of the water. There was a huge shadow there, like a man with a long nose and a bent head. If it had not been that I had only just got Robin to sleep, I would have screamed. I was sure it was Kankredin.

"That one-armed jokeman says my Robin is poorly," Uncle Kestrel said. He was rowing toward the door with a tiny light in his boat. Where my shadow came from, I do not know.

It did me good to see him. "It's no good going for mussels," I said. "The King's camp is by the mill-pond."

"I know that, my love," he said. "I came to see how you all did."

I knelt on the doorstep, crying a little, and told him about our travels, our King and the One. But I did not tell him about Gull. He thinks Gull died on the way.

"Kings and Undying are like that," said Uncle Kestrel. "They take no account of the trouble they cause. You make sure to keep Robin here until she's well. That's what matters. Is there any little thing I can get you from your house?"

"You're the only person in Shelling I love!" I said. "Did they break my loom as well as the roof?"

"Now don't get so fierce," he said. "They did not. They only took their feelings out on the walls and roof." Then he said something that has made me angry ever since. "I'm not excusing them," he said, "but you gave them provocation, you know, even Robin. You all knew you were different, and you acted as if you were better. It made for hard feelings." I was too angry to speak. "You want your loom brought?" he said, and I had to forgive him.

"And my bobbins and my shuttles and my needles and my spinning wheel," I said. "And don't forget my yarn."

"You're trying to sink my boat!" he said. "Sometimes you sound just like your aunt." But he brought them, every one, and my spindles, which I had forgotten to ask for. I have never seen a boat so packed with wool. The loom was perched on top. I had to wake Duck to help me drag it indoors. He could not think what I was so excited about, but I think Uncle Kestrel understood.

Since then I have been weaving, unless Robin finds the noise too disturbing. The King is amazed at my industry. Indeed, I am often very tired, though it gets easier and easier. But I am afraid Robin will die, and I weave to take my mind off it. I pretended to myself that when the coat was finished, Robin would be well, but she is not. Then as soon as it was finished, I dreamed once more that my mother was telling me to think. And I found I had it all to do again.

The morning I started this second coat, Duck lost patience with me. Lately, because he is so bored, he has been spinning for me, and he was at work outside by the millwheel, which has clumps of forget-me-nots growing all over it. "Of all the boring, stupid, gloomy people!" Duck said. He flung the spindle down and waved his arm at the sun-scattered brightness over all the green growing things.

"Look at it! Look at you! You're even worse than Hern!"

I burst into tears and said I hated the King.

"Who cares?" said Duck. "He's keeping Gull safe, and us safe from Zwitt. What more do you want?"

"It's all my fault," I sobbed. "I betrayed the One to him. And I made you leave the One in his fire when we should have taken him to Kankredin. If we'd had the One then, everything would have been different."

"You're just letting yourself be taken in by what the King thinks," Duck said. He took up the spindle and poked moodily in the ground with it.

"I know I didn't obey the One," I said.

"Yes, you did! Don't be a fool," Duck said, stabbing with the spindle. "The One *arranged* it that way! He wasn't strong enough to meet Kankredin. If we'd waited for him, he probably wouldn't have come out of the fire at all. The One alone knows what would have happened if Hern had poured water on it!"

"Stop ruining my spindle," I said. "Are you calling the One a coward?"

Duck looked sideways at me through his hair. He ties it back with a band, but it always falls round his face in white tendrils. "No," he said, and he squatted there, using my spindle to draw patterns round a clump of grass. He reminded me of someone. "The One is deep," he said, "like the River. Tanamil knows. He's the one we should have asked."

"So you understand it all?" I said scornfully. "Tell me."

Duck looked sideways again. "You wouldn't believe me unless you'd worked it all out yourself, anyway."

I knew who Duck reminded me of—Ked, the ungrateful Heathen brat, when he was lying. I wanted to throw him in the mud in the empty millrace for making fun of me. I shoved him over sideways instead, for spoiling my spindle, and went raging into the mill.

I was so angry that I took my rugcoat off the loom and carried it to the River door to read for myself, by my own account, that Duck was talking nonsense. First, I held it up and looked at it. It is a very handsome coat in gloomy colors, touched here and there with bright yellow and burning red. It is also very large. In the front the gloomy colors gather up the center into a shape, and that shape is the same shadow with a long nose and a bent head that I saw when Uncle Kestrel came. I turned it round hastily, when I saw it. There is a lightness on the back that begins from the time we met Tanamil. I did not see that the same shape was there at once. But it is. It is made of grays and sallow greens, which are harder to see. Across the neck of the long-nosed shadow, near the hem, runs a band woven in that expressive twist which Tanamil showed me. It expresses my terror of Kankredin and his soulnet. Nothing else goes right across the coat, except the place where I unpicked my long lament for my father. I do not think even Robin would see this unless I told her it was there.

I was so frightened when I saw that double shadow that I dropped the coat. My skin crawled, and I wanted to wake Robin. But I said to myself, I made this weaving. I wove in it that it held the meaning of our journey. No one is frightened of a thing they made themselves. Read it, Tanaqui, and find out what you meant.

I knelt on the floor, in the doorway, and read what I had woven. It took nearly all morning, even though there were places I moved over very rapidly, remembering what I had woven. It was comforting at first. Here were we all, Robin, Hern, Duck, and I, and poor Gull, being ourselves, and there was my own beloved River in his grandest time, being as usual a part of our lives. And I noticed many things. I have thought about them all these three days I have been weaving my second coat.

I had read down to the place where we found the cat Sweetheart when I could have sworn I heard a seagull cry. I looked up at the red, sandy Gull, beside my loom, first. Then I looked out over the leaf-speck-led green River. There were no seagulls near Shelling. I thought I had imagined the sound, from reading about the gulls on Sweetheart's island.

Then Sweetheart herself jumped down the ladder to the upper floor. Cats often appear when you think of them. It is one of their strange ways. Sweetheart was carrying a mouse. She jumped on Robin's bed to give it to Robin.

I knew what Robin would think of that when she woke. I got up to take the mouse away. And moving upright gave me a sight of the other bank of the River, just below the last house in Shelling. I saw Zwitt under the clump of hawthorns there—the may is over now— and another man moving to meet him, as if secretly. This other had darkened his light hair and further tried to disguise himself with a garish rugcoat—and a shoddier piece of weaving I seldom saw—but I knew him by his mauve pointed face and crooked mouth. He was Kankredin's mage, the one with *hidden death* in his gown. I could see the gown looped up under the dreadful rugcoat.

I dared not move while he talked to Zwitt. I was halfway across the dark room by then. And there was my coat, laid out in the doorway, in the full light above the River. Zwitt was nodding, talking eagerly, and pointing directly at the mill. He was telling *hidden death* where we were.

"Tanaqui!" Robin called out fretfully. "Sweetheart's put another mouse on my bed!"

"Ssh!" I said. "She does it because she likes you."

"Take it away," Robin said. "Take it *away*!"

"Oh, please shut up," I whispered. "Something awful's happened!"

The mage turned his crooked face toward the mill and saw my rugcoat. I saw his face change with fear.

He leaned out across the River, staring, as if he were trying to read it. As he was a mage, perhaps he *was* reading, with his eyes on two invisible horns, like a snail. I wanted to snatch the coat away, but I dared not let him see me. I stood helpless. Robin, who is no fool, even ill, lay quietly and stared at me as anxiously as I stared across the River. And at last the mage turned away downstream, and Zwitt went back toward Shelling. I took my rugcoat and hid it under Robin's bed, until I could finish reading it elsewhere.

I told Robin. I would like to weave a curse on Zwitt because of the panic and terror Robin has been in. She said we must get away at once. She got up and fell on the floor. I yelled for Duck, and luckily Hern came, too, and we got her back to bed. We are all very frightened. We know we should tell the King that the One says we must leave, but we are afraid Robin will die if we do. And as Duck pointed out, Robin's soul will be caught by Kankredin's net, which is just as bad as if he had caught Gull. We do not know what to do. Duck and Hern have kept watch these last three days, but the mage has not come back. We think he has gone to Kankredin. Hern says this gives us seven days or so. In that time I *must* cure Robin. I have inklings already.

As soon as Robin was settled, I set up new warps in my loom. This was because of the understanding that came to me when the mage was afraid of my weaving. When mages weave, what they weave is so. That is why his gown shows *hidden death*. That death, to whomsoever it was sent, *is* the very words that boast of it. It is the same with Kankredin's gown. The River is bound, Gull's soul endangered, and the soulnet set up by Kankredin weaving those words.

My weaving is a performing, too. I am sure of it. When I compare my close and intricate weaving with that of the mages, so loose, large, and crude, I know I am a greater weaver than they. Setting up my threads, I felt very vengeful and vainglorious. I meant to curse Zwitt, to weave that our King became serious and courageous, and then to say that Kankredin and his net crumbled into the sea. That is why I put in my wish that I could turn the Shelling people's feet the wrong way. I am quite relieved to look across the River and see that their toes still point to the front. I know why. I am like Hern. I need understanding. When I have woven my understanding, then Kankredin will have cause to fear.

This is what I must understand. Why is Gull's soul of such special value? Why is Robin so ill? And what is the One? These questions are all bound to lesser ones, such as what have Hern, Duck, and I sworn to the Undying that we will do? The answers all lie in my first rugcoat, and they are coming to me as I weave.

Robin seems calmer this evening. Before I read my rugcoat, I would have put her panic over the mage down to illness. She has not seen Kankredin. We have not told her much. But now I am sure Robin knows many things the rest of us do not. It is her birthright, as mine is weaving.

I can weave this, yet I get angry when Uncle Kestrel tells me that we gave offense in Shelling! It is not very logical. I read my rugcoat, and I remember, and I know that we all, even Gull, who is the most modest of us, felt and behaved as if we were special people. I think we are now. But the fact is I had no grounds to think it then. I had no business to set myself up. I am ashamed. I could almost apologize—no, not to Zwitt or Aunt Zara.

Here I stopped to light the lamp. Robin seemed asleep, with her yellow candle face turned to the wall. I shut the door to the River and read my first coat again. I do not blame myself about the One now. I see him roosting cunningly in his fire and contriving that I should appear before Kankredin in Robin's skirt, so that Kankredin thought I was of no account as a weaver. I think he arranged I should betray him to our King, too, and that we should be summoned to Kars Adon, though what his purpose was, I still have no idea. If I go back, I can even think that the One used Kankredin's power over Gull for his own end, to bring us to the Rivermouth. And I am certain that Tanamil delayed us until we would arrive as the floods went down.

Just beyond that place, when we first saw the tides, I looked carefully at my account of the Heathen girl on the roof. I noticed that Robin had not been herself even then. I tell hardly a tenth of what we all said— if I put in all Duck and I say, my rugcoat would be too large for a giant—but Robin says barely a tenth of that. But about that Heathen girl—I had left out what she was wearing. I jumped up to ask Hern.

The latch clicked and Jay came in. "My!" he said. "That's a beauty of a coat, lass. Who's the lucky man?"

I said I had made it to take my mind off Robin. True.

Jay glanced at the bed and saw Robin was asleep. He put his face down by the lamp and whispered, "When do you think she'll be well?" He had a significant twist to his face, but I had no idea why. I tried to keep my eyes off the jumping stump of his arm and did not answer. Then Jay leaned closer still and said, "When will she be well enough to listen to advances from an honest man with one arm? I think she likes me enough, and I want to be sure of her before it's too late. Understand?"

I could not think how to tell him what Robin thought of him. "Not really," I said, and looked at the floor because my face was so hot.

"The King," Jay whispered. "The King, little lass! The thought is shaping in his head that he has no wife, and he needs the power of the One. Has he never talked to you? Hasn't he mentioned that he needs an heir?"

"Did he mean he wanted to marry Robin?" I said. "It never entered my head!"

"Lucky for me you didn't understand him," Jay said. He was all merry with relief. "Speak to your sister for me—quickly, soon. Tell her I can't knowingly go against the King, so it's up to her to marry me before the King declares himself. You say that. Tell her she's the sweetest girl I know."

Then he went. I sat and stared at Robin's yellow face. She bounced up out of her pillow as soon as the door had shut.

"What shall we do about *this*?" I said.

"Jay wants the One," Robin said, "just like the King. Oh, I wish I was dead!" It was the first time she had said that, but I know she meant it. She plunged down on her bed, crying, and rolled about wretchedly, tipping the cats off.

"No, stop," I said to her. "I'm thinking of something. I almost have already." I dashed off to find Hern, as I had meant to before Jay came.

Robin called tearfully after me, "Tanaqui, I'm sorry. All I seem to do is complain at you. You're so patient."

Patient! If Robin only knew. "I've nearly hit you a thousand times," I called back, and went flying out into the blue evening.

Hern was sitting moodily against a tree. Beyond him the King's campfires sent merry streaks down into the water of the millpond. I could hear people singing. "Hern," I said, "when Gull and Father went to war, what did you swear to the Undying?"

"I said I'd free the land from Heathens," Hern said sourly. "Ha-ha! Go away."

"Oh," I said. I could not see what the One could make of this oath. Mine was easier. I had asked to be sent to war as a boy, and Ked had indeed taken me for a boy because I was wearing Hern's clothes. "Another thing," I said to Hern. "That Heathen girl on the roof who told us about the tides—what was she wearing?"

Hern scowled. "A sort of blue rugcoat— No. She couldn't have been. Heathens don't wear rugcoats. I don't know."

That was it. "Tanamil wore one," I said.

"Kars Adon would probably say he'd gone native," Hern said gloomily, showing where his thoughts were. There has been no news of Kars Adon since the broken bridge. "Go away."

I went away and looked at my rugcoat under the lamp. When Robin asked what I was doing, I said I was sewing it up and I would go to bed soon.

"I looked at it," said Robin. "It's beautiful. But why do you use that strange word for river? I keep thinking you're talking about the One."

It was like a great light cast. "Robin," I said, "I knew you'd help me!" She meant Tanamil's sign for the River. It is not unlike the sign for *brother*. I had often noticed that. Now I plunged outside for a handful of rushes from the millrace and wove them together furiously under the lamp. I wove the two signs of my own name: *Tan—aqui*. I weave it here to show. See: together, *rushes*; apart, *younger—sister*. Then I took more rushes and wove again: *Adon, Amil, Oreth*, the One's secret names. *Adon* is as much as to say *Lord*, the difference of a thread. *Oreth* I do not see so well. It is a sign for weaving, or knotting, but not the usual one. But *Amil* is *River*, all but a thread. I took all the rushes undone except that name and the front of my name and held them together in front of me.

So now I know. I have been weaving it until late at night because Robin is still too upset to sleep. And I still cannot believe that we are wrong and everyone else is right and the One is indeed the River. But I know what I must do. I must find Duck. He has the Lady inside his shirt.

|| 3 ||

Duck was nowhere. I took the lamp and went upstairs to bed in the end. And the first thing I saw was
the Young One, thrown out of my bed on the floor. I
rushed to pick him up. He is so worn and old that I
was afraid Duck had damaged him. Duck had thrown
him out. He was in my bed asleep. He says he prefers
it to sleeping in a tent. I held the Young One under
the lamp and made sure he was not broken. The light
made the smile move on his worn clay face. Then I
shook Duck.

"I'm not asleep," said Duck. He was in his maddening mood. "The King told me about needing an
heir, too."

"Then why didn't you come down when I shouted

for you?" I said. "I want to know what you swore to the Undying."

"Do you?" he said. I told you he was maddening.

"And I want Mother," I said.

Duck had thought he was the only one who understood. He was annoyed. "You can't have her," he said, and sat up against the wall with his arms wrapped round himself.

"She's my mother, too," I said. "I wouldn't ask if I didn't need her."

"You're not having her," he said. "I found out before you did, and she's mine."

I was too angry to argue anymore. "You selfish little beast!" I shouted, and jumped on top of him. We wrestled and struggled. "I need to talk to Mother!" I shouted. Duck at the same time screamed that the Lady was his and I was stealing her. Half the boards came off the trestles of the bed. We crashed to the floor. I heard Robin call out weakly from downstairs, and the door latch rattle as Hern came in to find out what the noise was. I had my hand on the Lady by then. Duck had my hair in both hands and was shaking my head about.

Then, through the noise we were making, we both heard the River door open below. Robin screamed. Duck and I stared at one another without moving, and Hern said, "I don't believe it! I just don't *believe* it!" just as he did at the net of souls. We heard light footsteps walking from the River door.

Neither Duck nor I remember how we got to the ladder. We were halfway down it before my mother reached the middle of the room. Hern was backed against the other door. Robin was upright in bed, with her hands to her mouth. And the River door was open where I had left it shut.

"What a disgraceful noise!" Mother said to Duck and me. "There's no need to behave like babies!"

I think the way she spoke did more to reassure us even than the cats. The cats had all jumped off Robin's bed and were rubbing purring round Mother's ankles. She bent down and stroked them. My mother is beautiful. She looks no older than Robin, but her face has more angles to it than Robin's and looks more delicate. Her hair is bushy, like mine, just as it was in my dream. But my dream did not show her huge eyes, deep and green as the River, and the long, long lashes round them.

"Lie down, Robin, love," she said. "It's all right."

"You came so suddenly," Robin said tearfully.

My mother smiled at her and at Hern. "I know it's hard to believe," she said to Hern. "Some things you can't see or touch are true, you know. Now what was all that shouting about?"

"Can I speak to you privately, Mother?" I said.

"I hoped that was it," said my mother.

"I want to talk to you as well," complained Duck.

"No, Duck," said Mother. "You go and make Robin's bed. It's all sliding to the floor. It's high time you did a bit to help, instead of leaving Tanaqui to do all the work. You've talked to me for hours already."

"Not properly, not with you really there," Duck said. "That doesn't count."

"Yes, it does," said my mother. She is a very firm mother. She would have been good for Duck. Hern grinned, because he thought so, too. "Don't go away, Hern," she said. "I want to talk to you afterward." Then she went back toward the River door, holding out her hand to me. She stopped on the way, beside my loom and the pink clay Gull. She put her hand to its cheek, smiling. Now, I had left the lamp upstairs. There was only the candle flickering by Robin's bed, so I cannot swear to it, but I think the small statue smiled. "Come along," she said to me.

I hung back on the threshold of the River. "Where?"

"Silly," said Mother. "I'll keep hold of your hand."

We stepped out across the River—I think. But things get so strange when you are with the Undying. There was a moon, and green light rippled through the trees, above and below us. I do not know if I walked on the water, or beneath it, or in some other place entirely. Certainly nobody saw us, but I remember seeing the square of dim light from the mill door to one side as we talked, and the lights of Shelling on the other.

"You've been thinking at last, Tanaqui," said my mother. "I don't suppose you can understand how it felt, watching you weave and willing you to stop blaming yourself and start thinking. I'd almost given up hope. I was telling myself that you'd put so much of the River in your coats, maybe that would do instead."

"Is it important," I said, "to put the River in?"

"Yes," said my mother. "But that is connected with the things I was forbidden to talk about when I married your father. You have to be very careful what you ask me, Tanaqui."

I had supposed some things were forbidden. My father was never talkative, but even he would have told us some of it had he been allowed to. I was prepared to be cunning. "Do you know about Kankredin?" I asked.

"I do," said Mother. "I was there with you. The mage *hidden death* reached him this evening. You have to move fast, all of you."

"We know," I said. "Are you allowed to tell me if Tanamil's a relation of ours? His name is Younger River, isn't it?"

"No. He is of himself," Mother said, to my great relief. "You have charge of him simply because he was bound when my father was bound. He has his name because he made the younger River—even more unwillingly than your grandfather made this one."

"Oh good," I said. "I was afraid he was going to turn out to be our uncle. I think Robin's in love with him."

"So do I," my mother said dryly. "That kind of thing seems to run in our family."

"Can you tell me how to call him?" I asked next. "Do I have to go to the watersmeet?"

"Any lesser stream will do," she told me. "But there's no need to scream like you did before."

That made me a little ashamed, but not much. I was too pleased, and too happy to have a mother again. I leaned against her. She was warm and solid and smelled, just faintly, of tanaqui. "I can't ask about the Undying," I said, as if I was talking to myself, "which means I can't ask if the One is my grandfather. But I know he is. Mother is his daughter. Are we—?"

Mother chuckled. It was like water in pebbles. "Don't get too cunning, Sweetrush."

"Can I ask your name, then, and how you came to marry my father?" I said. "You *are* the lady who haunts the mill, aren't you?"

"While Closti was a young man, I certainly haunted it," said Mother. "He used to come here to fish from the time he was Gull's age. And one day I met him by the millpond. 'My name is Anoreth,' I said, 'and will you marry me?' Anoreth means 'unbound,' Tanaqui—I can tell you that, since you are nearly there already. I suppose asking like that is more the kind of thing you would do than Robin, isn't it? Closti said he had seen me reflected in the water, often and often, and he was only too glad to marry me. But he was betrothed to Zwitt's sister. He had to give the coat back, and they were furious. So was Zara. And I was cast off by my father. That was when the mill was forbidden, through his anger. So when Duck was born, I should have died, but my soul was forbidden to go, you see. I had to ask your father to do for me what

Tanamil did for Gull. That way at least I could watch over you all."

It seemed a sad story to me. Now I know why Zwitt dislikes us so much. "Gull," I said. "Can I get Gull back?"

"Ask Tanamil," said Mother.

"I'll go and get him now," I said.

Mother kept hold of my hand. "Wait," she said. "Have a little tact, Tanaqui. Tanamil does not like to remember he's bound, for one thing. Then there's Robin."

"Yes, I know Robin knows things. She knew who Tanamil was," I said. "What shall I do, then?"

"Sleep on it," said Mother. "Kestrel could lend you a boat to get Robin away in."

We went back together through the River door after that. Mother kissed Robin and Duck. Then she took Hern out into the wood and talked to him. I think she knew Hern's mind would not take walking into the River. Hern will not say what she said to him, but he is much happier now.

But I disobeyed Mother this very morning, the day after Mother came. Robin woke around dawn. She was pale and damp-haired and iller-looking than ever.

"I wish I could die quicker than this!" she said.

I had not seen before that Robin *meant* to die. I was appalled. "Kankredin—" I said. I was too sleepy to say more.

"I know all about his net," Robin said. "I shall be

expecting it. Duck says quite a lot of souls get through."

"How do you know how fat your soul is?" I said, but I did not stay to argue. The fact is, I do not know what I should do without Robin. I raced upstairs and came back past Robin with the Young One in the sleeve of my rugcoat. "I'm letting the cats out," I said. They were mewing about because they thought it was morning. I went out with them into a white fog. Everything was dripping softly. I looked anxiously into the mill-race. The sluices from the pond have been closed longer than Robin has lived, but there was a trickle of water down there among the rushes and forget-me-nots.

I climbed down there and put the Young One on one of the slats of the millwheel. "Tanamil," I said, "Younger River, will you please come here? We need you very badly."

I felt very silly. The flaky stone image did not change or move. When I heard someone coming along the millrace behind me, rustling the wet plants, I felt so foolish that I jumped round to stand in front of the Young One.

It was Tanamil who came along the race, out of the wet whiteness, with fog drops clinging to him all over. My mother did right to warn me. He gave me a doubtful, distant look, as if he had never seen me before. "Did you call me?"

At first I could not think what to say. Then I remembered how we should have asked him the right question, and only Robin did. "Last time," I said, "I should have asked if you were the Young One, shouldn't I?" And I moved so that he could see the Young One on the millwheel.

That was a mistake. He looked aside from the figure, almost shuddering. "That's true," he said, polite and distant. "I am the Young One."

He was so unhelpful that I burst into tears. I am getting as bad as Robin. "Boohoo!" I said, just as if I were a baby. "It's not *my* fault you quarreled with Robin! And now you're like this, and the King wants the One, and so does Jay, and we can't get away from Kankredin even, because Robin's trying to die! Boohoo!" And I went on boohooing until Tanamil shook me.

"What did you say about Robin?" he said. I think he had to say it several times. When I cry, I can hear nothing but me.

"She's trying to die," I said.

"What nonsense!" he said, looking very angry. He came out of the millrace, pulling me almost as fiercely as I pulled the brat Ked, and crashed in through the mill door. Robin sat up with a shriek. "You look like an old woman!" Tanamil said to her. I think he could have been more polite. Just then I found Duck beside me, staring at Tanamil. He looked at me, and we shut the mill door and went to sit outside in the fog.

"I've been wondering whether I dared get him,"

Duck said. "But I was afraid she hated him for being of the Undying."

"We're of the Undying, too," I said. "We descend from the One on both sides."

"I don't know—we feel suspiciously human to me," Duck said. "Maybe it's just our souls that are different."

"I must ask him how to get Gull back," I said.

"He told us," said Duck. "He said take him up the River to the One, only we didn't understand." He was in a much more obliging mood than the night before. He said, "I'll take him, if you like. I have to go. I swore to the Undying—it was after Zwitt said the River was angry and we weren't to pasture our cow with theirs, remember?—and I swore to see every inch of the River so that I knew more about it than old Zwitt."

"I see," I said. "That means the One wants us to go. We must get hold of a boat again."

Soon after that we were so cold and so curious about what was going on in the mill that when the cats came and mewed at the door to be let in, we opened it and went in with them.

Robin was sitting up cross-legged on her blankets, eating—stuffing, in fact—and her face was pink again. Tanamil was passing her things from the table, which was loaded with finer food than even the King has. He smiled at us and invited us to eat, too. Then he looked at the cats, and there was a fish on the floor for each of them. The mill seemed filled with peace and pleasure. I think Tanamil always brings this feeling. But on that occasion it was more than that; it was Robin, too. I was right. They are in love, and they mean to marry. Robin is almost well again already.

Tanamil assured Duck that the food was *not* an illusion, as Hern said. He has the power to bring anything which is on the banks of streams and lesser rivers, even from the far south, where very few people live. As he was saying this, Hern came in. He was carrying the Young One, accusingly. "Who left him—" he said, and he saw Tanamil.

I was afraid Hern was going to be angry. He was not, but he was awkward. I think Mother talked to Hern of Tanamil. All the same, it has taken Hern most of the day to get used to him. And Tanamil would not look at Hern because Hern was carrying the Young One and Hern did not understand. I had not realized how much Tanamil hates being bound. He hates it so much that he will not speak of it. His face loses all expression when you ask him, and he looks like the image of himself.

"Amil Oreth is bound deeper than I am," was all he would say when I asked. Robin told me angrily to leave Tanamil alone. At that Tanamil seemed to relent a little. He did not speak of himself, but he said to me, "Adon has a double bond to bear now. In the first place, he was cheated by a woman, and it was his own fault. In the second place, he was already bound, so that he could not use his full strength against Kankredin."

We have had such a good day. Hern has neglected the King entirely, and we have sat about in the mill laughing and trying to make plans for getting away up the River without the King or Zwitt knowing. Tanamil sits with his arm around Robin, as happy as we are, and Robin must have eaten more today than she has in the last month. Anything she fancies is instantly on the table. My only regret is that we are not allowed to have Mother here, too. Because of the One's anger when she married my father, Tanamil is not allowed to speak with her. Tanamil is not going to risk the same thing happening over Robin. They are going together to ask the One's permission to marry.

Now the fat is in the fire! Now I see why Tanamil so hates to be bound. I should not have disobeyed Mother. But at least the main fault this time is Duck's, not mine. I will tell it in order.

We were very happy, sitting in the evening sun from the open River door. I had a feeling Mother could be with us like that. I brought my weaving up-to-date and then turned to sewing up my first rugcoat and clipping the ends. Tanamil came over to look at it.

"What made me think I could teach you anything?" he said.

I was very pleased, but I said, "You told me two very useful things," and I showed him the band of expressive weaving at the back, where we went to Kankredin.

"I was there with you," he said. "I knew you would

need me; he was almost too strong for me, too. It was lucky he sat down and that you repeat his spellgown broken here. Did you realize it would have made another bond on us?" I had not realized. It is a frightening thought. He told me that he had left when Kankredin said we could go, knowing Duck could take us through the net; it was Tanamil who brought us through it the first time, of course. Robin had told him never to come near us again. The quarrel had been far worse than I had known. I think it was good of him to help us at all, though he says he was thinking so hard of us all, and Robin particularly, that it is a wonder there is anything growing on the banks of streams anywhere.

Then he said, "I was as bad as Amil over Cenblith, but I hope I shan't need to expiate my folly the same way."

"By being bound, you mean?" I said.

"No," he said. "By fire. When it was almost too late, he found how to cheat the woman who cheated him and made her promise to put him in a fire every year. Every fire reduces his bonds by a fraction until they can be broken."

He looked so sad, saying this, that it came to me that it must hurt the One to be in the fire. I had not seen that before. And we put him in the fire so happily. "Did you know the One is golden now?" I asked Tanamil.

"Yes," he said. He picked up my rugcoat and looked at it. "That means his bonds can be broken," he said.

"What are you telling me?" I said. You have to ask

the Undying clear questions. They do not tell you things properly.

Tanamil put the thick folds of my weaving back on my knee. "We call this a spellcoat," he said. "I think you should take it to the rising of the River. But I am not certain. You are making a thing here which is beyond anything I know. I dare not risk spoiling it by—"

Here came the disaster. The King came in with Jay, to pay his evening visit to the One. His pouched eyes twinkled merrily at Robin. "My dear young lady! Looking better at last! Restored to health and considerable beauty, isn't she? And how is my golden gentleman?"

Tanamil was standing against my loom, but the King did not see him, nor did Jay. Hern, Duck, and I made faces of astonishment at one another. Robin was too busy with the King to look at anything. She said the One was safe and she was feeling better today.

"Good! We shall be able to move on again," said our King. He circled the room, passing in front of Tanamil without knowing it, and seemed arrested at the sight of my rugcoat. "My dear fluffyhead, this is beautiful! Now I see the purpose of all your industry. I call it truly delicate, my dear!" He took the rugcoat off my knee. My hands went out to stop him, but he whisked it out of my reach. I thought Tanamil might have stopped him. But Tanamil stood as if his hands were strapped to his sides. The King held the rugcoat against himself. It was far too big for him. As I said, he is a small, plump man. But his eyes twinkled delightedly at Robin. "Your sister has made a royal coat for our betrothal, my dear. When shall our wedding be?"

When I think of all our faces, I could almost laugh—though it is no laughing matter. We were all horrified, but Duck was worse even than Tanamil. He stared at the King as if he was a monster and backed away into a corner. As for Jay, he was worse even than Duck. He staggered, as though the King had hit him, and glared at me. I see now that he thought the coat was for him.

"But, Majesty," I said, "the coat's too big!"

"We can turn up a hem or so," the King said, "at the bottom and round the sleeves. I must admit, fluffyhead, that either you miscalculated or you were thinking of another man." The sideways twinkle he gave Jay made no doubt about who he thought the man was. He bowed to me. "Thank you for my coat. I shall salute my bride-to-be." He took Robin's hand and kissed it. He can be very courtly when he pleases.

Robin dragged her hand away. She looked ill again. "I haven't agreed yet, Majesty."

"Nonsense," he said. "This coat is agreement. Shall we marry tomorrow? The headman in Shelling can do the business."

Robin looked desperately at Hern. Hern said, in a cracking voice, "Majesty, we object to Zwitt. You'll have to find another headman to marry you." Hern says this is the law. He says he was lucky to remember it because his mind was spinning.

"Well, frankly, I don't care for Zwitt either," the King said, readily enough. "We note your objection, brother-to-be. We'll use the next headman we find. I'll go and give orders to pack up and leave. Sleep well, my young lady." He bundled my coat under his arm and took it away. Jay went with him, looking as if someone had hit him in the face.

He left us in uproar. Robin was in tears, with Tanamil embracing her. I found I was making the noise old women use at funerals. All my work misused and gone. Just as I had understood its nature and how to use it. Hern was demanding why Tanamil had not stopped the King.

"I'm bound!" Tanamil cried out. "I'm bound, I tell you! I have to do what the King wants."

"Do you mean you can't marry Robin now?" Duck asked. He was very shaken.

"Not unless the King changes his mind," said Tanamil. I think he was near to tears, too. Robin put her face in her hands and wept that he was not to leave her, ever.

Duck stared at them guiltily. "I'm sorry," he said. "I told the King about Jay last night. He cheated. He promised me he wouldn't let Jay marry Robin."

"And he hasn't," said Hern. "Don't you know better than to trust the King, you stupid little—"

"Don't *fight*!" said Robin. "We've all we need without that!"

‖ 4 ‖

THE KING IS LUCKILY not very passionate over Robin. His main wish is to move on. I am weaving this amid the bustle of clearing up to go. The King visits Robin frequently, to remind her she is to be Queen, I think. You would think it would make her ill again, but Tanamil is with her, and she gets better every day. The King is unable to see Tanamil, but he has no illusions about Robin's feelings. He has detailed ten men to watch us night and day.

"Not Jay, I'm afraid," he said to me. "He's not a man I trust in affairs of the heart. But my bride must have a proper bodyguard, fluffyhead."

The bodyguards watch by five and five. Robin has no chance of getting away. Hern says we must stay with her. All I have been able to do is to insist that the One wants us to travel by River. It was not easy. The King has shown a desire to overrule the One. "A King is awfully exposed by water," he says. "We shall be a big slow target for every Heathen crossbow. Are you quite sure our golden friend really wants us to?"

"Yes," I said.

So the King has taken all the boats from Shelling. Zwitt stands scowling at us across the River, but I think it serves him right.

Tanamil has recovered his spirits again. In spite of our worries, we are flooded with his joy and pleasantness, which makes me feel very strange sometimes. I could not think why Tanamil was so cheerful until he came to me and said, "This second coat you're weaving—does it describe the first coat?" I said it did. He smiled and said, "Then I think it may be used instead." I can see he has set his hopes on this. If this coat has power to unbind the One—and it might, since it holds my understanding—then Tanamil will be unbound as well, and he can marry Robin whatever the King says. The difficulty is that the King will marry Robin as soon as he finds another headman.

Sometimes I think Tanamil lacks hardness. I would move against the King if I could, bound or not. But then I think of the way his arms seemed pinned to his sides when the King took my rugcoat away. I think Cenblith did her work well.

* * *

Robin has given me the One. She has Gull and the Young One, and Duck has Mother. We have moved a day's journey up the River, beyond the great marshes.

We went in thirty small boats, watched by all Shelling standing on the bank. We were in the marsh most of today. The King's men shot ducks there, which they are cooking for supper. Everyone is scratching because of the mosquitoes. We nearly lost the King in the marsh—a thing I would have been glad to do at any other time, but not when Hern was in the King's boat. Our boat is large and slow, because it carries the bodyguards, and we lost sight of all the rest. It is not surprising. The pools and channels of the marsh change every year with the floods, and the whole is hung with slight blue mist. There are warm springs underneath, which make the mist and cause flowers of all kinds to riot and tangle at this time of year. Every so often the mist and flowers part to show a smoky blue mere. Each time we searched the bleary water for signs of the other boats, but there was nothing but the jump and scuttle of wild creatures.

One such mere was covered with silver birds. When our boat broke through the rushes, they rose into the haze on bent wings. I cried out in fear. "Seagulls! Mages in disguise! Shoot them!" The bodyguards looked at me in consternation.

Tanamil smiled and stood up. He was sitting unseen with Robin. It is as if their troubles have increased their love. They cling together. When he stood up, the seagulls flocked to him and flew calling round his head, while the eyes of the bodyguards rolled sideways, and they muttered of spirits.

"They're only gulls," said Tanamil, and he sat down. The birds flew away. "There are storms at sea. They talk of great waves."

I felt foolish. After all, this could be a sign from the One that Gull will be restored to us. But now that I am sitting weaving on the bank, removed from the peace Tanamil brings, I think the gulls were telling of Kankredin's anger. I am very glad that we are moving at last.

I have had no chance to weave for three days. At least Robin is not Queen yet, for which it seems we must thank the Heathens.

That morning after the marshes we were woken by numbers of people hurrying along the bank among our tents. The cats hid in my blankets because the people had dogs with them. I sat up and stared through the tent flap at the confusion among the willow trees. There were children and donkeys, men and dogs, and everyone waving lights and shouting. The King had come out with his face creased and crumpled with sleep. But even with the King asking them, the people would not stop or answer clearly. We gathered that Heathens were coming up behind. They shouted that the whole countryside was in flight and fled on.

"That's no reason to give up common politeness!" said the King. "Move!"

We took to the boats and packed and folded our

things as we rowed. My loom was nearly left on the bank. I asked Jay to make them load it, but he walked away. Tanamil carried it to the boat. Nobody noticed in the confusion.

Since then we have traveled as fast as oars and sails and men dragging on the bank could take us. We traveled till light was gone. As summer is here, that is many long hours. And when we landed, they were tired and cross and would not unload my loom.

The River is shallower after the marshes, and more winding. It is crowded with willows for a day's journey. In one place a willow had fallen in the floods and lay, still living, across the River.

"Oh, curse this River!" the King said. "He seems to be doing his best to thwart me!"

Our boat was alongside his. Unkingly though it is, I think our King is frightened. I told him the One would not like to hear him speak like that.

"Then tell him to behave more like a benefactor," the King said. "Are you sure he really wants us to go this way?" He looked at me almost pleadingly. Hern looked at me, too. Hern does not understand why Duck and I are so set on going by water.

I told the King I was sure. "Why am I so sure?" I asked Tanamil, while the bodyguard was busy shoving at the willow to squeeze us underneath.

"Your father's people bound us," Tanamil answered out of a mass of pointed willow leaves. "Your father's people know how to unbind us." Why do the Undying never tell you straight? I long to ask Mother a few more cunning questions, but I am not allowed to talk to her when Tanamil is there, and he never leaves us.

The willows stopped after a day. The River, no longer eye green but clear gray, hurried toward us down a valley of green banks. We saw white birch trunks above us and green bracken. Beyond that there were mountains. Some have a dazzle on their peaks which hurts your eyes. One of the bodyguards told me it is snow. It is no good asking Tanamil anything anymore. He is too taken up with Robin. Duck has gone to join Hern in the King's boat. He says all this love suffocates him.

In places where the valley was wider there were humped bridges over the water and houses nearby, built of stone. We found most of them empty. But yesterday the King said, "Ah, people! We shall have our wedding now." Robin looked piteous.

But the people all ran away up the hillside among the bracken. Jay stood up and shouted to the headman that the King needed him.

"Heathen!" the headman shouted as he scrambled upward. He pointed down the River. "Heathen! Run!"

There were no Heathens. We could see some miles down the valley there, and there was no one. Tanamil smiled. I think it was his doing. I see I have wronged him, saying he was soft. He is not powerless to work indirectly against the King, and he does. But he is mad if he thinks he can delay the King's wedding until I have this coat finished. It is barely half done.

However, the King was in a great panic. He said

we must put off the wedding and hurry on. So we have come, at a furious speed, to this place. We have only halted here because of a great downpour of rain. The green hills around us were shaded white with it, and large hailstones fell. It was too fierce even for the King's hurry. We went blindly into a wider valley, where the River runs as a small tossing lake, and there we dimly saw a group of trees. The King angrily ordered us to take shelter there. Under the trees there is an old barn or boathouse, built of big gray stones. Here we all wait, while the King paces impatiently up and down and the rain pelts dimples into the water.

They would not at first bring my loom in. Jay, who used to help me in such things, is not my friend anymore. I had to make Hern ask the King. I am sad about Jay. I have wronged him, too. It was not the One he wanted. It was Robin. I do not know why I am so unready to believe that people can love Robin. I have seen Jay look at her just as Tanamil does. And now Jay will not forgive me.

The King could not understand why I should want my loom. "Why, in the name of the golden gentleman, fluffyhead, do you need to keep on weaving coats?" he said.

"I have to make one for Robin, too," I lied. "We always do that in Shelling."

So my loom was carried in, wet as it was, and set up in the doorway. I am sprinkled with rain as I send the shuttles back and forth, but I do not mind that.

"It's all wet, wool and all," the King pointed out.

"The way we prepare and spin our yarn," I said, "that does not matter."

He looked at Robin, who had taken some of the wet yarn to spin for me. Then he frowned at me, in his quizzical way. "Fluffyhead," he said, "it usually matters. Wool shrinks. Sometimes I suspect you of— Do the Heathen have lady mages? I think you may be one."

"No, Majesty," I said. "That I am not."

"Then can you swear to me that you're not making all this pother of weaving on behalf of some other man?" he said.

My heart grew large and bumped a little, but I said, "This is for no mortal man, Majesty."

Then he was satisfied in a dissatisfied way and went to the doorway to look at the rain. Hern sat with his back against the stones of the doorway and scowled out, too, beside my loom. We look out across a rocky, shivering sort of lake. Almost at my feet, rain popples among rushes. I keep looking up and out between rows because this is as near as I have ever been to real mountains. They ring us round, high green shoulders, higher brown shoulders, and headlike peaks which are blue and black and veiled in swimming clouds. Now that the rain is slackening, I can hear water rushing and shouting down all round. It is the sound of streams that run in every groove, some so distant that you see them as a white smear, like a snail's path; others I can see leap and spray.

"I don't see us going much farther by boat," the King said, and turned away, more satisfied.

I think he is right. We shall have to leave the River. The River comes to the lake in a sort of cleft, between two high shoulders of brown hill, and I think it is a rushing torrent there. Up above the cleft, in the highest and blackest mountain, I can see a smear of white that must be our great River at its rising.

Hern has just noticed.

So much has happened since then, and so little time to weave it in.

As I was saying, Hern looked down at the rushes by our feet. "The tide's turned. Look at it running the other way."

I leaned around my loom. The small blobs of foam and twigs that had gathered against the rushes were moving slowly past the bank, toward the rushing water where the River comes down the cleft. It seemed to me that Hern was right for a moment. "But the tide doesn't run up in Shelling," I said.

We looked for Tanamil to ask him. He was leaning over Robin as she spun, over on the other side of the doorway. He did not notice us. Lovers!

"Jay!" Hern called. "Does the River have tides up here?"

Jay came and looked at the water. He ignored me. "No. Tides stop at the Red River. That must be an eddy. The waters run pretty swift out in the middle and force the edges backward. See?" The stump of his arm leaped as if to point.

In the middle of the lake we could see angry waters standing in peaks with the force of their running. I could not quite believe Jay. It was churning there, like the tides do.

And a churning came among the rushes at the doorway. It was all spouting whiteness there. Hern and I were soaked. In the midst of the whiteness Mother stood, with her head and shoulders out of the water, quite dry. She was angry.

"Tanamil!" she said.

Tanamil jumped and put out his hand as if he could push her away. "I can't speak to you," he said guiltily.

"I *must* speak to you," Mother said. "You were trusted to watch, Tanamil! Take your mind off Robin and attend. Kankredin is coming. He and his mages are halfway up the River already, rolling my waters up before them as they come."

"But—" said Tanamil. "Without Gull?"

"Zwitt told them Gull is my son," my mother said. "After that Kankredin guessed how he had been tricked. He'll take Hern or Robin instead. He knows where they've gone. Take that spellcoat back from the King, you fool, and show Tanaqui what to do with it at once!" My mother turned, in a surge of whiteness. A great white swan went beating off across the lake, making the air ring with its wide wings.

I think the King and his men had seen Mother as a

swan all along, rearing and hissing at the water's edge. They called to one another to put an arrow in it, saying swans were good to eat, while Mother talked. As I recovered from the shock of what she said, I heard Jay saying, "If I had my other arm, that would never have got away!" I do not like Jay anymore.

Duck came to crouch between Hern and my loom. "Where is the coat?" he whispered.

"In the coffer in the King's boat," Hern whispered back. "I'll create a distraction of some kind. Then you and Tanaqui go and get it."

I looked over at Tanamil. He nodded urgently, but he held out his hands with the wrists together, to show he could do nothing himself.

"Be ready to go as soon as no one's watching you," Hern whispered.

While we waited, I could hardly even pretend to weave.

Duck, however, jerked a handful of rushes from the water and wove them idly into a small mat. He looked bored to tears.

We did not wait long. The King noticed how pale Robin had gone. She had dropped the spindle when she saw Mother and sat staring straight ahead, twisting her hands together. I could see her mouth saying, "Oh no! Oh Mother!" I think she thought it was her fault that Tanamil had neglected his duty. She would not speak to Tanamil when he bent and whispered to her.

"Cheer up, pretty one!" the King said. He came and

pinched Robin's cheek. "It was only a swan," he said. "You sweet, timid creature! I really am quite fond of you, you know."

"In that case," Hern said, jumping to his feet, "why don't you get on and marry her?" He marched round my loom, denouncing the King. "You talk about it enough, but you don't do it! What are people going to think? I can't have my sister gossiped about!"

He said a great deal more. Hern can be very eloquent when he chooses. I wish I could have stayed to hear it and to watch the King's face. It was the first time I have seen our King entirely without a smile. But by the time I had slipped round my loom and among the rushes outside, the King had recovered enough to wrench the smile back onto his face. "My dear boy," he said. "My dear boy!" Each time he said it, Hern thundered louder and harsher.

"Robin's name has been sullied!" he was shouting as Duck and I hurried among the trees. Tanamil was in front of us, beckoning. "My family's name is mud!" Hern roared, and we could not help giggling.

"I hope the King won't take Hern too seriously," Duck said as Tanamil slipped down into the King's boat. It did not so much as dip as Tanamil went aboard it, but it plunged for Duck and me.

"The box is locked," said Tanamil. He stood by the King's beautiful carved chest, looking helpless.

Duck laughed and cracked his thumbs. He has double-jointed thumbs. He holds them upright and they hop about, looking as beastly as Jay's stump. He did it now, and the carved lid of the King's coffer hopped in sympathy. I took hold of the lid, and it lifted, pouring rainwater over my feet. "How did you learn to do that?" I said.

"Tanamil taught me," said Duck. Tanamil was out on the bank again. He laughed.

My coat was folded on top of golden things. As I snatched it up and bundled it into my arms, I saw enough plates and goblets encrusted with red and blue stones to have bought our whole country. I turned to follow Tanamil.

Jay landed heavily in the end of the boat as I turned. I saw from his face that he disliked me even more than I knew. He looked at me as Zwitt did. "You thieving fiend's child!" he said. "Your brothers are just as bad. What are you all playing at now?"

"Nothing," I said. "The King has to be married in this coat. I'm getting it for him."

"Liar!" said Jay. "Heathen liar! You may fool the King, but you're not fooling me anymore. Give us that coat. And you can hand over your golden statue while you're at it!" I do not know how Jay knew I was carrying the One in the front of my shirt. He must have been watching me for days.

"Into the River," Tanamil said to me from the bank. I glanced at him and saw he had his pipes to his mouth. I tried to plunge sideways over the side of the boat. Jay's one hand fastened itself into the spellcoat and jerked me back.

"No, you don't!" he said. "You're coming to the King."

I did not care that Jay has only one arm. I bit the hand that held the coat, and I thrust at him in the way Tanamil taught me. We both went over into the water in a spout of splashes. It was bitterly cold. Jay howled and struggled. I had not known he could not swim.

"Duck!" I yelled. "Rescue Jay!"

At that moment Tanamil's pipes sounded. It was a breathy scream, like seagulls, and a crying, like an old woman at a funeral. I felt as if I had been taken out of my head and put somewhere strange and terrible. There was a long streak of light and, in that streak, smooth sliding. Then Tanamil and I were standing by the lake, surrounded by mountains as before, but everything was calm and empty, with a whiteness to it. There were no boats tied to the trees, and the trees stood as if in fog. Yet I could clearly hear a great splashing and large tricklings. Out of nowhere Duck said, "You're all right, you fool! Put a leg over the side. It's your own fault for making Tanaqui bite you."

"Ough! Oughgurrouch!" went Jay's voice.

"What do I do now?" I said to Tanamil in the whiteness.

"If you're ready, you go farther down," Tanamil said. "You must make your way against the River's current to its source."

"Aren't you coming?" I said.

Tanamil shook his head. He had that expression which was no expression. "I can't come any deeper because of being bound," he said. "Besides, I couldn't help you when you come to the source. It has to be one of your father's people who unbinds us. I must go and find Kankredin. Your mother was quite right."

"Oh," I said. I was very disappointed. I suspected he wanted to be with Robin again.

:|| 5 ||:

Tanamil played his pipes again. It began as a shriek, but it passed to a hurrying, sobbing sound and died away. There was the streak of light and the sliding. This time I knew it: It was the same as when I had looked into the floods at night, not knowing the River was so high. It does not last long.

When I saw things as they really were, I was in the bed of the River, between high shadowing banks, among a flood of another sort. This was all people. People hurried past me in a shadowy crowd, more and more, coming always from the left and hurrying away to the right. My ears were assailed and irritated by the clatter of their feet. The clattering never stopped, yet it was oddly hard to hear. The people never stopped, and they were hard to see. Only when I looked at a person, and turned my head to keep my eyes on him or her as they hurried by, could I see them clearly. In this way I saw four men of our own people, a Heathen woman, two Heathen boys, and a girl about Robin's age who was neither Heathen nor of our people. All were strangers to me. And always they hurried by between the shadowing banks, on and on.

"Gull's rushing people!" I heard myself saying. "These are the souls of dead people. Now I know. The River is everyone who dies."

Speaking like that took too much of my attention. Next thing I knew, I was hurrying with the crowd, panting with haste, on and on. The only difference between me and the rest was that I was still clutching my rugcoat and feeling the One bumping heavily in my shirt.

Nothing seemed to stop me as I hurried. I did not think of stopping, until I saw light shadowy movements in the far distance. The hurrying of the people became broken and hesitant. There was an uneasiness, and we ran waveringly. Then I could see that people were turning about ahead, and some came past, going the other way. They were unwilling and kept trying to turn round. The clatter of our feet was in confusion.

Up till then I had run as one does in dreams, not asking why a thing happens. But now I stared ahead and tried to make out what the light shadows were. I saw huge glassy shapes striding toward me. They were transparent, but green and wavering, as if they were made of water. Though they were still far away, they were enormous and striding fast. I could not see what happened to the uneasy crowd as they met the glassy giants. But I had a sense of nothing beyond them, and I thought I heard among the faltering clatter of feet a voice crying out in despair. It sounded like my mother's.

I was terrified. I tried to turn back and struggle away from the glassy beings. It was most difficult to do. The hurrying was still all the other way, and it swept me with it. I cried out for help.

Then somebody was calling me, above on the bank. "Tanaqui, Tanaqui! Where have you got to, Tanaqui?"

I looked up, expecting my father. I think that, all along, I had been expecting to see my father among the rushing souls. I saw, running along the bank and peering down at the crowd, a fair-haired young man in a faded red rugcoat. He was fiercer and sturdier than Tanamil, but he had a joyful look which was like Tanamil's. I clung with an elbow to the rocky bank and gaped up at him.

"There you are at last!" he said to me. "Mother told me you'd be here. You mustn't go that way. The mages are down there. Come up here on the bank." He held his hand down to me.

"Gull!" I said.

"Who did you think I was?" he said, and pulled me up on the bank.

"But . . . you're grown up," I said. "Are people's souls always grown up, then?"

He was annoyed. "I'm not my soul. I'm all of me. Come along. We've got quite a way to go."

He hurried off along the high bank, the other way to the way the people ran, and I did my best to keep up with him. It was very stony and uneven, quite unlike the smooth trodden ground of the Riverbed. "Why are you grown up?" I panted as I stumbled after him.

"Because I was born five years before you were," he said, striding along. By this time I was falling steadily behind. Gull realized and turned back. "Sorry," he said. "You're loaded to the thwarts, aren't you? Whatever have you got?"

"My rugcoat," I panted. "But it's the One that's really heavy. He went gold, you know."

"I'll carry the coat for you," he said, and took it out of my arms, which was a great relief. "It's a beauty," he said when he had it. "It must be the best you ever did. What have you got it for?" Then he smiled at me. "I'm terribly glad to see you, Tanaqui."

Gull says things like that only when he means them. I was truly pleased. I explained to him about the rugcoat as we walked up the bank above the hurrying multitude of souls, to the perpetual soft patter of their feet. Kankredin's glassy mages were out of sight behind. Everything was shadowy. Gull was the only bright thing I could see. I suppose that should have told me he was not just a soul. But in spite of being with us all the time, Gull did not know anything of our adventures. He told me that he could barely remember the part where he was with us in his body. As I explained, I found it hard not to say, "But surely you remember Robin was ill!" and "You must know what our King is like!"

When I came to the end, I said, "Now what do you think I have to do to unbind the One?" and Gull did not know that either. "I hoped you'd know that," he said. I was thoroughly dismayed.

"But you must know!" I wailed. "I can't ask anyone else here, because it's got to be one of our family that does it!"

"Yes, I know. We bound him; we unbind him," Gull said. "Don't get worked up. Let's think." It did me good to have someone calm like Gull. That is one of the things I have missed. "You've got the One," he said, "and you've got the spellcoat that shows you finding out how Kankredin caught the One and then me. And Tanamil says it was lucky you didn't see all Kankredin's gown— That's it, Tanaqui! The spell is broken in your rugcoat! You try putting the coat on the One in the presence of Oreth!"

In that place, when Gull spoke that name, its echoes rolled in the Riverbed. The hurrying people halted, and their white faces looked up.

"I'll show you where his source is," Gull said quietly. The echoes died, and the people hurried on.

"I can't get used to the way things are the same and not the same," I said. "The One is not the River. Is he this golden statue?"

"He was before the River, and he made it," Gull

said. He paced seriously and frowned as he tried to explain. Gull is not a thinker like Hern or Duck. "Making the River, he was bound as the One. He is the River, in a way, or its source at least."

"But the River is people's souls," I said. "And it's water, too."

"It's all those things," said Gull. "But . . . well, if anyone's really the River, I think Mother is."

"Mother!" I exclaimed.

"I can't explain," said Gull. "But I've talked to Mother a lot. I don't think the One likes it, but he doesn't stop me. Mother's not bound, you know, but she's in disgrace for marrying Father. She's told me all sorts of things. You wouldn't believe all the strange places and strange sorts of Undying there are in the land. When we're unbound, I want to go and see some of them. That's what I want to do. I shall have much more fun doing that than what Hern's going to do, I can tell you!"

I remember looking down at the Riverbed while Gull said this. It was narrower by then—a sort of rocky split—and there were far fewer people hurrying along it.

"What *is* Hern going to do?" I said.

Gull laughed. "I'm not telling. You won't believe me."

"Do you know what we're all going to do?" I asked eagerly. "What about me?"

"That I *can't* tell you," said Gull. "It would be terrible bad luck on you. But our Mallard's going to be a mighty mage—I'll tell you that. We go down here. Take careful hold. The rocks are slippery."

The sides of the split were wet. It was the first moisture I had seen in that place. I would have expected moss or mold or green things growing, but there was nothing but wetness. I went down, clenching my hands on rock and feeling my feet slide. Gull came after me more easily, but I saw he was taking care, too.

When we were down, the rocks of the sides were high above our heads, and between them was dimness. Though the place was dark, there was a yellow-greenness everywhere, by which we could see. I looked back down the narrow channel. It was empty where we stood, but there were people behind us, two or three or more, always hurrying away from us. I never saw where they came from. In front of us were rock and an oddly shaped dark hole.

"We go in there," said Gull.

He stooped and went into the hole. I edged in after him. How I felt is hard to explain. I was not frightened. I still went as you do in dreams. Yet there was a terror that was like part of the dream which, had I been really dreaming, would have woken me screaming. Gull moved to one side, and I followed him. It was soft and silent inside the hole. As soon as I moved from the entry, I could see. It was a cave, where the light fell greenish on the rocky back, and it fell in the shape of a figure with a bent head and a nose that was neither straight nor hooked, but both at once. I looked at the hole we had come in by. That was the same shape. Both were the shape of the shadow in my rugcoat. The cave was wet. Drops of moisture stood like dew underfoot and overhead, but the dew neither dripped nor trickled. It was a deep empty silence we stood in.

"Where—where is the One?" I whispered.

"Here," Gull said. "Can't you feel? This is all there ever is."

It was perplexing. I could not put a coat on nothing. If I had been alone, I would have got as bad as Robin and started weeping and wringing my hands. But Gull was there, and he was not worried. In the end I took the golden image of the One out of my shirt. He was so small that it was ridiculous, but there seemed nothing else I could do. I placed him carefully on the dewy rock, so that he stood in the center of the green man-shaped light. "Give me the rugcoat," I said to Gull. Gull did so, and I placed the coat over the golden figure so that the head showed but the rest was heaped round with my weaving. I spread the cloth out and stood back to watch.

Nothing happened.

"We haven't got it right!" I said. "What shall we do? We've got to do something before Kankredin gets here!"

"Wait," said Gull. "Feel."

There was warmth growing in the cave. Almost as Gull spoke, it grew from dead chill to the heat of a body. Gull and I both sweated, in big drops, as if we were part of the walls of the cave. Steam gathered about us.

But that was all. We stood and waited in the heat, but nothing else happened. The small golden figure still stood swamped by my rugcoat. The green-yellow light was unchanged, except by the haze of steam.

"What shall we do?" I said.

"You've done something," Gull said thoughtfully. "It's never been warm here before. But I don't think that's enough. There's something else we have to do, I think—and I simply don't know what."

We stood again, and still there was nothing. At last, I could bear it no longer and cried out. "Grandfather!" I cried. "Grandfather, show me what to do!"

There was a green sliding in the cave. I could not see the rocks or the One in my rugcoat, but I could see Gull. He was bent and pallid and out of shape, like a person swimming underwater. Then I could not see him. I was in a still white place, with water roaring and rushing nearby. The sliding came again. This time a chilly wind came with it. I shivered, but I was glad of it after the heat of the cave. After that I was out on a cold hillside in the light of a golden evening. The first things I saw were heavy rain clouds, swimming away to the west in a green sky and limned with a dazzle of gold. Green turf sloped sharply from my feet. Somewhere to my right, water poured shouting downward, tolling an echo like a bell. And beside me more water ran and spread on the turf from steep rocks behind, which were smoking like a fire.

I felt heavy tears dragging in my nose and eyes, but I stopped them. "My grandfather," I said, "has turned me out. I call that ungrateful." Then I looked at my hands, thinking I was carrying my rugcoat again. I was not. My hands were gripped on a bobbin wound with a dark yarn that glistered faintly. And I could feel that the heavy weight of the One was missing from my shirt.

I felt desolate. I knew how Robin felt that morning we woke and found Tanamil had left us. I knew how Hern has felt, knowing he had failed. But neither of them had just lost Gull for a second time. I walked with my strange bobbin across the soaked and steaming grass, not caring or noticing that my clothes were dry where they should have been wet, and barely grateful for the cold wind on my face. I told myself I was going to look down at the thundering water I could hear.

I believed I could throw myself down it, but I had to stop before I came to the brink of the turf. It was too high and too steep. The green country and the purple hills spread like the whole world below and seemed to wheel sickeningly. Almost at my feet was the beginning of our River. It poured in a white cataract from my turfy shelf to somewhere far, far below. It roared as it fell, and everything beneath it was lost in floating smokes and small drifting rainbows. Beyond, and away below, I thought I could see the lake where we had sheltered from the rain, as a bright lozenge laid in the wheeling steepness. I had to take my eyes away and fix them on my tall black shadow, lying nearby across the turf.

"What did I do wrong?" I said. I have been so proud and so sure of myself, ever since understanding came to me in the old mill, and now I saw I had prevented myself understanding truly by being so proud of my own cleverness. "But what about Kankredin?" I said. I tried to look out into the country below, to see if Kankredin was to be seen, but my eyes blurred. It was all green and blue and dizzying.

I looked at my shadow on the turf. There was another shadow stretched out beside mine, longer and large-nosed. I could not move.

"Grandfather?" I said.

His voice is like the sound behind the sound of the waterfall. "Thank you, Granddaughter," he said. "You have been a great help to me. You took Kankredin's hands from my throat."

"Then what didn't I do?" I said.

His answer came after a pause. He sounded sad. "Nobody asked you to do anything—beyond what your family has always done. And I was not very kind to your mother, after all."

"I know," I said. "But Closti—my father—wasn't in the least like Cenblith, you know. You might have forgiven her."

He paused again before answering sadly and hesitantly, "I am very devious, Granddaughter. You—you would not be here now if I had."

It came to me that my grandfather was not only bound and sad, and weighted with shame and loneliness, but even uncertain how to talk to an ordinary person like me. I had not thought it was possible to love him until then. I wanted to turn round and look at him, but I did not dare. I looked at his shadow and said, "Grandfather, tell me what I have to do to unbind you. I want to. It's got nothing to do with Kankredin or Mother or even Gull. It's for *you*."

Again the pause. "That makes me . . . grateful," he said. "If you mean that, Tanaqui, perhaps you could think of the end of your first coat, where you speak of Kankredin. In what manner did you weave that?"

"In the expressive way Tanamil taught me," I said.

"Then," he said, "think on to the second coat now in your loom. You tell of meeting with your King and what he told you of me. Do you use the same weave there?"

"Yes," I said. I had been in such awe of our King then. And I saw the coat clearly in my mind as I stood there, and my expressive weaving of the King going right across from selvage to selvage. "Of course!" I said. "You were bound twice! By Kankredin and by Cenblith." Then I did nearly turn round to look at him, but again I did not dare.

"It was my own fault," said my grandfather. He spoke musingly, as if he spoke to himself. This is how he must have spoken alone, for many centuries. "I can't ask anyone to unbind us because it was my fault. The first time I was a fool. The second time I was a fool, thinking that I was about to be rid of the first bond in time to welcome my people back. I let Kankredin take me unawares. I knew Kankredin. He has inherited my gifts, but it was too late when I saw that he has put them to the worst possible use."

"Kankredin? Is Kankredin of the Undying?" I said. I could not help interrupting.

"He descends from me," said my grandfather. "All the people you call Heathen descend from me. They went from here, and now they have come back. Kankredin is like you—two lines meet in him—but he has misused his inheritance, and now he wants to take my place."

"Can you stop him?" I said. By this time I was shaken with the urge to look round and see my grandfather, but I could not do it.

"I can stop him if I am unbound," said my grandfather. "That I promise you."

I could not resist turning round. I was so frightened of looking that I slithered down on to my knees with the bobbin clutched to my chest. I think I gave a whimper of panic. But I turned round.

Kars Adon was standing there, casting a long shadow on the turf beside the blob of mine. He smiled awkwardly at me. There was nobody else there. "You mustn't be frightened," Kars Adon said. "I made them keep out of sight. I was afraid you might go over the edge if we all came."

I DO NOT KNOW if it had been the shadow of Kars Adon all along, but I think not. I do know this, however: At the bottom of my mind I must have been thinking of Kars Adon as much as Hern had. I was so glad to see him standing there alive that I burst into tears and took hold of his hand; it was cold, and all knuckles, as I remembered from before.

Kars Adon, being such a stiff, polite person, was naturally hugely embarrassed. He twisted his hand out of mine and stepped back. "Please don't cry," he said. Then he thought he had been too chilling, and he said, "I am very pleased to see you up here. We wondered what you were doing."

"Didn't you see the One?" I said. "I was talking to my grandfather."

Kars Adon looked at me with an oddness he was almost too polite to show. "There was no one here," he said. "Who did you think it was?"

"He's called Adon, like you," I said, "and Amil and—"

"Hush!" said Kars Adon. He was very awed. "You mean our Grand Father was here?"

I nodded. I was crying again, to think the One had gone away without my seeing him.

"Then is that why the water coming out of the hill is suddenly smoking like this?" Kars Adon asked.

"Doesn't it usually smoke?" I said, sniffing busily.

"Not while we've been here," he said.

I was cheered by this. "Then it shows I've done something," I said, and my crying stopped.

"If you feel better," Kars Adon said, "I think you should come with us. We are having to move from here. Kankredin is coming up the River, they say, in a great wall of water. As he hasn't sent word to me, I'm assuming he's my enemy, too, now."

"He is," I said. "He wants to be King himself."

Kars Adon twisted his mouth at that. "Thank you. I should have seen that. I could have seen that even when my father was alive, now that I think." He fidgeted a moment with the hem of his cloak, and then he said, "I owe your family a great debt. If it had not been for your brother, I would still be crouching like a mouse in the hem of Kankredin's gown, dreaming of—of glories . . . and risking getting trodden on. Hern made me see how ridiculous that was."

Hern would be glad of that, I thought.

"You'd better come to our camp," said Kars Adon. "I can show you some gratitude now, at least."

"Oh, but I can't!" I said. "My weaving's down in our King's camp, and I have to get it and finish it before Kankredin gets here. You wouldn't believe how important that is!" I took a look over the edge of the turf, down to the tiny slip of the lake below, but I had to snatch my eyes away.

"Is your King down there?" Kars Adon asked, suddenly very eager. I thought he had not noticed my talk of weaving at all, but I found later that I was wrong.

"Yes," I said. "We got to the lake down there this afternoon."

Kars Adon was delighted. "Then that alters everything," he said. "We stay here. I shall send someone down to talk to your King, and they can ask for your weaving then. I think Hern would say that was the right thing to do. You come with me."

He wrapped his cloak around him against the wind and walked away up the turf. He walked with a strong limp; I had been right about that. When I did not come with him at once, he called to me, "Are your brothers with the King?"

"Yes," I said.

"Then everything will be all right," he said, and walked on.

I caught him up easily because of his limp. As we walked round the mountainside together, I asked him if he had been wounded.

His face was pink, and he shook his head. "I was born this way," he said.

In the trees beyond the shelving turf, we were met by six lordly-looking Heathens. They had that grave, anxious look Heathens always seem to have, but I think they were truly anxious. One asked, "Shall you give orders to strike camp now, lord?"

"I've found a better way to settle our troubles," Kars Adon said. "The native King is at hand, and we shall face Kankredin together." He motioned me to walk with him and limped swiftly down the hillside, with the lordly ones following. From the conversation they had as we went, I gathered that the lordly ones had been trying to persuade Kars Adon to leave the place for days, because of Kankredin. They were frightened white by Kankredin, even more than Robin is. It began to give me a sense of how strong Kankredin is, their fear. But it was also quite plain that it stuck in Kars Adon's gorge to flee from Kankredin. He had been looking for an excuse to stay, and he had found it in what I had said.

The lordly ones kept saying that prudence was safety, and who could face the mage of mages? Kars Adon limped on without answering until we came to a trodden path leading out from among the pine trees when he flung over his shoulder, "I was prudent once before and nearly lost the clans. Now I shall trust to our Grand Father." That silenced them.

The Heathen camp spread beneath us. It was very large. Numbers of flags flew over many tents in one of the most favored valleys I have ever seen. It was warm, facing south, and flowers grew there in such profusion that they scented the evening.

"As I promised your brother, I have mustered all the clans that remain," Kars Adon told me, and his chin lifted. I could hear imaginary trumpets. "I want to make my kingdom in this dale." I did not blame him. It is a beautiful place, and no one else lives there.

When we came down among the tents, the first thing I saw was a group of dark boys in rugcoats making up to three Heathen girls in clinging dresses. They were being very polite about it—offering to carry the girls' waterpots and so on—but I was a little shocked. We went round a tent, and there was the same thing in reverse. Some very forward girls in rugcoats were coaxing away at two Heathen boys to give them a ride on their horses.

Kars Adon saw me look. "Your people have been coming here for days now," he said, "fleeing from Kankredin. I made treaties, as I told you I would. You think Hern would approve?"

I did not know what Hern would think. Treaties sound very grand, but the practical result is an awful lot of giggling and a very strange camp. Polite, quiet Heathens looked at us without seeming to look. People of my race crowded and stared. Some of my people were not at all clear they had made a treaty. Kars Adon was hissed by some, and some sat about staring and made no attempt to look after themselves. Most of these, Kars Adon explained, had been too near Kan-kredin. "I think he has hurt their souls," he said. "They think they are our prisoners. We have to feed them." He sighed. "I often wish that your brother was here to persuade them."

We went to Kars Adon's tent—he had found a great white one big enough to act a play in, from which his garish flag flew proudly—and there we had supper. It was plain food, nothing like the food our King insists on, and confusing. Heathens have the whole meal out upon the table at once, but you do not help yourself. Everything is carried to you by boys. I saw Ked among the serving boys, but he kept to the other end of the table. He is still terrified of me.

I sat eating with a most peculiar mixture of feelings. I was shy, but I felt at home in a way I never did with our King. When I realized this, I began to think I was a traitor, and yet, I told myself, the camp was full of my people, and my grandfather had placed me where I would meet Kars Adon, as if he had intended it. Kars Adon spent the whole time telling me of his plans, and this was oddest of all. "You do agree?" he kept saying. "Do you think Hern would like that?" It was all Hern. It is strange to think that Hern has made as big an impression on Kars Adon as Kars Adon has on Hern. They did not talk together long. But each has gone away thinking deeply of the other and, as it were, trying to live up to what he imagines the other to be. Kars Adon seemed to me to credit Hern with ideals that Hern never had. But how can I tell? Hern has certainly credited Kars Adon with the same, and here was Kars Adon doing his best to achieve them.

After supper Kars Adon sent his lordly ones to the end of the tent and said he must talk privately with me. "Would your King agree to a parley?" he said. "If I offered him a treaty, would he agree to face Kankredin with us?"

The way our King was placed, with fifty men and Kankredin coming up the River, I could not see he had much choice. "I think if you sent someone he could trust and listen to," I said. I did not think he would listen to one of the lordly ones.

"I know the very person," Kars Adon said, and he sent lordly ones in all directions to find this man. "Then you spoke of weaving," he said to me. He was very respectful. Of course weaving to his mind is the mages' art. "Should I ask our messenger to bring you this weaving?" he asked.

"Oh yes!" I said. And then I told him why it was so important. It was something I had never dreamed of myself doing. But he had been open with me, and we were both children of the One. He was equally in danger from Kankredin. I told him of the first coat and how it had loosed Kankredin's bond. "But I don't know what I have to do to unbind him from Cenblith's," I said. "Have you any idea?"

Kars Adon was at his most awkward at this. He wound his fingers in his cloak and twisted about. I think the reason was that he had hoped for just this from my weaving and was ashamed of making me tell him. "I know nothing at all of magery," he protested.

"But nobody knows about this," I said. "And you can look at it fresh."

I think he was flattered. He considered. "What did you give our Grand Father in the first coat?" he said.

"Kankredin's spell broken and our journey down the River," I said. "The second one starts with the King telling us how the One was bound and what happened when we came up the River."

Kars Adon thought deeply. "Would it be," he said at last, "that you are to give him back his bonds and the entire River with it? And perhaps the story of how you discovered this?"

You know, he is right! I knew it as soon as he said it. This is why I am weaving this now. But it is still not quite the whole story, and I know I must go on.

I had not finished thanking Kars Adon for his cleverness when someone came up to us saying, "They say you want something from me, young lord."

We looked up, and there was Uncle Kestrel bending his shaking head to Kars Adon in the most respectful way. "Uncle Kestrel!" I shrieked. I jumped up and hugged him.

"Ah, now, I thought it might be you in our midst," he said. I put a kiss on his beak of a nose. It came to me that my grandfather looks a little like Uncle Kestrel, which is a good thought. It seems that Uncle Kestrel and all the rest of Shelling were forced to run away from Kankredin the day after we left. The River flooded backward and drowned most of the houses. Zwitt was so frightened that he made them go by land to the mountains, while we, because of the winding of the River, took much longer to reach this place.

Kars Adon told Uncle Kestrel to go to our King's camp and arrange a meeting as soon as possible, and he gave him strict instructions to bring my loom and yarn back with him. Uncle Kestrel was a little surprised to be chosen, but it was a good idea. Robin would believe him, and the King would believe Robin. "That weaving," said Uncle Kestrel. "I do nothing but fetch her that weaving." He agreed to go. He keeps his independent manner, but he thought the world of Kars Adon.

I had a lumpy bed that night in a tent with some Heathen girls. They chatter just like our girls when they are on their own. They told me that Kars Adon had asked every one of our people who came to his dale whether they knew the family of Closti. And when Uncle Kestrel came, he had exclaimed, because Kars Adon reminded him so of Hern. Kars Adon spent several hours asking Uncle Kestrel all about Shelling and about Hern. The girls were a little shocked that their Adon, as they call him, should be so interested in natives. I was pleased. I thought all was going well.

In the morning, however, I heard that Uncle Kestrel had not brought my weaving. Our King had made conditions. He agreed to talk and named a place, but he said he would exchange my weaving for the One. He knew I had the One.

"But I haven't got him anymore!" I said to Kars Adon. "I gave him back to himself."

"That won't matter," Kars Adon said. "We can explain. The important thing is that he has agreed to talk." He was overjoyed at that. He set out soon after dawn with me, and Uncle Kestrel and seven of his anxious lordly ones, to go down to the place the King had named, near the lake.

So it was that I have seen every inch of the River, and my coats between them contain it all. As we climbed down past the waterfall, I made myself look at it, although the height and the noise made my head turn round. It streams down hundreds of feet, not wide, but with enormous force, into a great rocky basin beneath the mountain. We climbed down to it over moss and hanging ferns, perpetually wet with the clouds of spray. That day Kankredin was so close that the basin had become a place of white waters, where the fall wound back on itself, up and round, as if it were trying to climb the mountain again. The din was enormous, and there were rainbows at the edge of the winding water as big as rainbows in the sky. Everyone stared at it, shaken. No one liked to say the name of Kankredin, but he was in all our minds.

Beyond that the water boils down to the lake through a curving ravine, in a chain of basins as blue as the eye of a Heathen, and white bubbles fight up through it. The ravine opens into a grassy space just before it reaches the lake. There, between slants of rock, the King was waiting. They were before us, not having had far to come. We came there feeling deafened. Even there the noise was loud. I could not think why our King should choose a place where we could hardly hear ourselves speak.

He was sitting on a stone, smiling at us. He even smiled at me. My loom was behind him, between Hern and Jay. Hern seemed to try to smile at me, too. In spite of what Duck said, he was sure I was drowned until Uncle Kestrel came. But I could see there was something else on Hern's mind. As for Jay, he half closed his eyes and gave me a look of detestation which I find it hard to forget.

Our King did not get up. That was to show Kars Adon he was usurper and invader, which was true enough. Kars Adon bowed to him politely. Our King bent his head, twinkled, and began to shout the names of the important ones with him. The first was a stranger to me, an agreeable-looking man in the rugcoat of a headman.

"This is Wren," bawled our King. "And this"—he pulled Hern forward—"is Hern, my young brother-in-law."

Brother-in-law! I thought. I stared at Hern. Hern heaved up his shoulders, spread his hands, and looked "Tell you later." But I did not need to be told. Wren was a headman. Robin was a Queen. Poor Robin. Poor Tanamil. Then I thought: But they hadn't got my rugcoat. I think it's unlawful! I missed the first part of what was said because of this. When I listened again,

Kars Adon was leaning forward, shouting earnestly into our King's face.

"We can't afford to be enemies," I heard above the thundering water. "We must make a treaty and unite against Kankredin."

"Treaty?" shouted our King. "You come to my land, kill, lay it waste, dispossess me, and then you bleat of treaties!"

"Things are different now," yelled Kars Adon. I lost his voice in the noise. It came to me in fragments: ". . . make amends . . . proud future . . . kingdom together . . . one tongue . . . same Undying."

Our King's voice carried better. "Who cares about all that? That child Tanaqui stole Oreth from me. I want the One back. She can have her weaving in exchange for the One."

Kars Adon was pleased the King should talk of the One. "Our Grand Father," he yelled, pointing a finger at my loom, "is the most urgent thing we must talk about."

"How dare you shout at me!" thundered our King. "Have you got Amil?" He looked at me and knew I had not got the One. It must have shown in my face. He stood up. I see now that it must have been a signal, though at the time I simply thought he was angry.

Next I knew, the King and everyone except Hern had snatched swords from beneath their rugcoats. I had never seen fighting before. It is swifter and more beastly than you would believe. The worst of it was,

Kars Adon, Hern, and I stood stupidly aghast, not believing our King's treachery. Before we moved, three of Kars Adon's lords had lost their lives, and most of the rest of the King's men were jumping down from the rocks where they had been hiding. Uncle Kestrel was hobbling frantically round us, with Jay slashing at him as he ran. Jay impeded our King, or Kars Adon would have died that first second. The King had to make a second stroke at him, and his sword moved to do it as swift and deadly as a snake.

Hern screamed, "You promised me not to!" and tried to get in front of Kars Adon. The King's sword sheared Hern's rugcoat half away. Kars Adon tried to step back. Hern fell into me and, as we went down, I heard the King's sword meet Kars Adon's chest. It was the most awful noise I have ever heard, dull and sticky. The same noise came again. I had glimpses of more Heathens with crossbows. Kars Adon may not have suspected treachery, but someone had. I think it was Arin, who fetched us from the island. The King fell just beyond me, choking, his face mauve and smiling a grin of pain. There was a crossbow bolt in his neck. And Arin stood above us, crashing swords with Wren, the headman, glancing down at our King in satisfaction, until they were both knocked aside by Uncle Kestrel, who toppled over with Jay on top of him. One of them was breathing even more dreadfully than the King.

"Grandfather!" I screamed. "Help!"

The answer was like a skirl of sheer anger, shrieking

above the thunder of the falls and the rasp of the fighting. I looked up and saw Tanamil on the rocks above us.

Tanamil had been very unhappy. His hair was a wild yellow cloud, and his rugcoat smeared with mud. I could see misery in his face, even through his anger. He was very angry. His pipes screamed with rage and struck across our ears like terror. All round me, people fell apart from their enemies, staring and shocked. And the pipes screamed on, modulating to a wail and down to sobbing. The heat and the shock died out of us. We began to stir sheepishly, and Hern and I climbed to our feet. I noticed that Tanamil seemed to be looking to the rocks behind me as if someone directed him. I turned. But it was not the One. It was Duck. Duck was crouched there, playing as Tanamil played, with that intent and irritable look you have when you are doing something which is almost too difficult for you. And Tanamil was directing Duck.

To the piping of both, even the noise of the falls grew quiet. Tanamil stopped playing and stepped to a high rock where everyone could see him.

"Stop behaving like beasts!" he said. We all winced. Tanamil angry is a great one of the Undying, without question. Like Gull when I first saw him on the bank of the Riverbed, he was more alive than the rest of us below. Unseeable strength came from him like hammerblows. "Attend to your wounded," he said, "and then attend to your real enemy. The mage Kankredin is nearly here."

Everyone knew Tanamil for what he was. The Heathen hailed him as Tan Adon. A number of the King's people murmured names: Tanoreth, Red One, and the Piper, to name a few. I had not known he had so many names. But Tanamil ignored their murmurs and came down to where Wren, the headman, was bending over the King. The King was not breathing.

"Who did this?" Tanamil demanded.

A shadow fell across the King, of a hawk-nosed man. I whirled round. It was not the One. It was Uncle Kestrel, heaving aside Jay's body as he got up. I was sad about Jay because I would never be able to make him like me again. But I was glad Uncle Kestrel was alive.

"Tanamil!" Hern said. He was desperate.

We all turned to where Kars Adon was dying, with his hands pushed hard to his chest, and blood running from one side of his mouth. Hern and Arin were kneeling beside him. Tanamil pushed between them and raised Kars Adon, very gently, so that he could see us all. "What is your will, lord?" he asked, as gently as he had lifted him.

Kars Adon looked at no one but Hern. "Hern," he said. I wondered how he could speak at all. The effort heaved his chest, bringing blood between his fingers. "Hern, was it the King's sword did that to you?"

Hern looked down under his own arm at the slashed ruin of his rugcoat. He was bleeding along his ribs. He was surprised to discover it. "Yes, it was," he said.

"Then," said Kars Adon, "we are blood brothers."

He laughed, and pink froth came from his mouth. "I meant to tell you so much," he managed to say. Then he pushed himself up with his elbows, so that he could see Tanamil, Arin, Wren, and all the rest of us standing round. "This is my will," he said, "all of you: that Hern is King and Adon after me, and that all the clans obey him."

Kars Adon passed into death so smoothly then that we could not tell when he did so. He spoke, and there was no difference to him, but he was not alive. After a moment his hands slipped from his chest, and we knew he was dead. I have asked the One many times to help him get past Kankredin in the River of Souls.

Tanamil laid Kars Adon down, and Hern looked angrily at Arin. The anger was because there were tears in his eyes. "I can't do that—rule the clans—can I?" he said.

"Someone must," Arin said. "It was his will, and you are very like him."

Tanamil said, with some bitterness, "You're the King's heir, too, since this morning. Accept it, Hern. There is a great deal to do."

: 7 :

After that the day was all hurrying, coming, going, meeting, and mourning. Tanamil seized a word with me in the confusion. "What happened?" he said. "Something came about, but not all. I find I can reveal myself to mortals, yet I had no power to stop the King's wedding. Was something more needed?"

"Yes," I said, and I told him what Kars Adon had said.

"I thought you might need to weave again," he said.

"But I think it's more than that," I said. "The One left me with this bobbin of yarn. What do I use it for?"

Arin came just then, to take Tanamil to the camp of the Heathens. "Your mother can tell you that," Tanamil said, and he left.

I snatched a word with Hern. "The King married Robin?" I said.

"Oh One!" said Hern, and covered his face with his hands. "It was my fault! I made him so ashamed, and all I wanted to do was to cover up for you. The trouble was, I said it in front of everyone, and he felt he had to marry her. Then Jay came in soaking wet, saying you'd run off with the One and were lying drowned for your sins, and the King was so furious that he swore nothing would stop him marrying Robin. He had them dragging the lake for the One. And Robin was too upset about you to bother what the King did. Then Uncle Kestrel appeared. The King went wonderfully calm after that, and I suppose I should have suspected he was up to something. But Tanamil had disappeared, and Duck and I had our hands full with Robin. Wren arrived around dawn. He had his whole village with him, and they were too scared to stop at first. The King made Sard shoot one of them. So they stopped. They were terrified. They say there's a wall of water half a mile high coming up the River. The King said we'd all move when he was married to Robin, but then he made them wait to look after Robin while he went to meet Kars Adon. He took Wren and me to make sure the rest all stayed. It's not been fun, I can tell you. Then Tanamil! Tanamil turned up during the wedding. He went dashing out across the lake, tearing his hair and yelling, and Robin began crying again. It was terrible. It's all terrible, Tanaqui. I can't be a King, can I, Tanaqui?"

He had wanted to say that most of all. "Gull knew you were going to be," I said. "He wouldn't tell me because he thought I'd laugh. But I wouldn't have laughed. Gull doesn't know how much you've changed."

"Being with the King has taught me what *not* to do, if that's what you mean," Hern said, but it made him happier. He wanted me to tell him what had happened to me, but I was not sure he heard it all. They kept asking things, and he had to hurry away before I had finished.

I found Duck brooding up on the rocks. "Isn't fighting beastly?" he said to me. We talked of that for a while. Then Duck said, "Old Smiler married Robin after all, just this morning. Did you know?"

"Yes," I said. "But I'd taken the rugcoat. What wedding clothes did he wear?"

Duck laughed. "Nobody knew you had. Remember that mat of rushes that I made?"

"Duck!" I said.

"I told you I was going to be a magician," Duck said. "I've got quite good at little things like that. Peacepiping's much more difficult. I thought I was going to let Tanamil down when we started. Anyway, I put that mat in the chest, and everyone thought it was your spellcoat. The King wore it. Nobody knew. At least Hern knew, but he was too upset to say and Robin did, of course, but she kept looking away because she hates people to look silly."

"But, Duck, I don't think the wedding was legal!" I said. I was thoroughly shocked.

"It was all right if the headman did it," Duck said grumpily. "And don't you dare tell anyone. Without that wedding Hern hasn't the slightest right to be King. So keep your mouth shut."

Duck is quite right, of course. I have not told a soul except to weave it in my second rugcoat.

By then a certain order began to appear in the coming and going. The bodies of the two Kings and the others who were killed were laid on the broad grass beside the lake. Wren, the headman, went round the lake to the barn among the trees. When he got there, Kankredin was so near that waves were standing high in the middle of the lake and its water was forced over the lowland. Wren found the barn flooded. Our cats were up in the beams, spitting at the water. Wren's villagers and Robin were up on the hillside above, and Wren brought them back round the lake to the falls, where I was still standing by my loom, wondering what I ought to do.

Robin is no different, in spite of being a Queen and a widow, though she was wearing her best skirt. She burst into tears when she saw me. She says she had known I was not drowned, but she had not been able to believe it. We went down to look at the King. You would not have thought Robin could cry over our King. But she did.

"You didn't *like* him!" I said.

"I know. I didn't treat him well," Robin sobbed. "Nothing treated him well. He wasn't the right man for what he was made to do."

I think Robin is right. But I was glad Tanamil was not near. He would have been hurt.

Tanamil was all this time up at Kars Adon's camp. I am glad he was there. If Arin had gone alone to the camp with news of our King's treachery, there would have been bloodshed, and Hern would have died in it before he could do anything. As it was, Tan Adon, as they call him, came in majesty to the Heathens and bore witness that Kars Adon had named Hern as his heir. Even so, the Heathens from the camp came down beside the falls with black looks and weapons ready. My people whom Kars Adon had sheltered came, too. But it was noticeable that they kept apart, with those too weak to fight sheltered in the midst of them.

Jay is not dead, by the way. While Robin and I were watching the people coming down the falls, Hern and Uncle Kestrel were laying Jay with the other bodies. And Jay sat up, rubbing his head. "I might have known you'd get the best of it, old-timer," he said to Uncle Kestrel. Then he looked at me. It was almost his old, joking look. "I've been sent back from a hurrying host of dead people," he said, "with orders to keep you safe, my lass. There are some glass giants at work down the River. It looks as if they'll be here by nightfall."

Uncle Kestrel thought Jay's mind was wandering. I knew it was not. "He means Kankredin," I said to Hern.

"I was afraid he did," said Hern. He lifted his heel and hacked at the grass with it. "Now I have a chance to do all the things I swore to do," he said. "And I don't think I *can*."

The people from the camp arrived and gathered by the lake. Our people went to stand with Wren and his villagers, near the lake. But the Heathens stood up among the rocks and planted their flags there.

"How shall we do the Adon's will?" a lordly Heathen called out mockingly to Hern.

Hern was very pale. I could see him shaking. He stood out between the two crowds, among the bodies, all on his own. I had expected him to look small there, and I am still surprised that he did not. Hern is thin still, but he has grown as tall as Gull. When Tanamil came to stand near him, the two were the same height.

"First look at this," Hern said, pointing to the corpses. Everyone was quiet. The noise from the falls meant we had to listen very carefully. "These," Hern said, "are the bodies of two kings. They were killed in senseless hatred, when both had lost nearly all they had. Someone is coming up the River who knows of this, and it pleases him very much. This will make it easy for him to suck out our souls, and the soul of this land, and rule us as his slaves. He is coming in a wall of water. And he is nearly here." He pointed down the River, across the lake.

Our people by the lakeside swayed all one way, like grass in the wind, away from the water. The Heathens stood firm, but their crowd was white with faces staring across the lake. The current set it in banks of water, churning toward us, and the space by the lake was flooding as Hern talked.

"This morning," said Hern, "one King married my sister Robin, and the other named me as his heir. This gives me a title to lead all of you against Kankredin. I did not ask for it, and you may choose again later, if you want. But for the next three days I must ask you to fight as one people against our real enemy. The same flags shall fly over us. The same Undying shall guide us. We shall none of us run away. We are going to hold these falls behind us to the death."

Heads swung uneasily to look at the rearing white falls. Everyone shifted with infirm resolution.

"We shall do it," said Hern. "For one thing, we shall lose our souls, anyway, if we do nothing. The main thing is that we have a way to win. My sister Tanaqui can weave against Kankredin, spell for spell. She can unbind Oreth, our Grand Father, so that he can rise and crush Kankredin. She can save us. But she must have time. We must hold Kankredin while she weaves. If we can hold him for three days, we have won."

So Hern did understand about my weaving. I admire him for grasping it so quickly. I did not think he would because it is not reasonable. But I never foresaw that it would all depend on me. I am very frightened. I know how Hern feels.

"If this is any comfort to you," Hern said, looking at the stricken faces by the lake and the grim ones up on the rocks, "the chief power of the mages is that they can take our souls. Everyone is right to be afraid. But Tan Adon, Lord of the Red River, will make you each a talisman which will keep the soul within your body. You can wear that and go into battle with confidence."

Tanamil, for an instant, looked as if he could not believe his ears. But as eyes turned to him, he smiled and nodded.

"So," said Hern, "will you all follow me—just for three days?"

There was the most nerve-racking pause. Hern sat down on a piece of rock. I think his knees gave.

Then Wren stepped out from among our people and went on one knee in front of Hern. I like Wren. "We'll follow you, me and my people," he said. That brought other headmen struggling through the crowd, one by one, and they knelt, too. Zwitt was one of them. Only believe that! He looked very grudging, but he was scared stiff. I think Hern's talk of talismans tempted him.

As the number of headmen increased, the Heathen lords realized they were being outdone. There was some hasty whispering among them. I am not sure that all of them believed Kankredin to be their enemy. But the will of Kars Adon was a powerful thing. All the Heathen flags dipped together, stood, and dipped again. A great shout went up. "Hail Hern Adon! Hail Hern King!" Arin tells me this is the custom among the clans. So, when the last headman went on one knee, both sides were pledged to Hern. I think Hern was near tears, because he scowled so.

After that our King was buried by the lakeside and mourned properly, although the grass was being covered in water while the mourning was done. I saw Aunt Zara among the wailers, but she would not come near us. But Kars Adon was carried up to the head of the falls and buried where the smoking waters of the One's source run across the green turf. Tanamil said it should be so. I can see the grave beside me as I weave. I look at it often and hope that we will be able to complete his dreams for him.

Before we came up here, I overheard Tanamil whisper to Hern, "Why did you promise them talismans? There is *no* way to keep a man's soul in his body."

"Yes, there is," said Hern. "If the man himself believes it's going to stay there. That's how I kept my soul when Kankredin tried to get it. I'm sorry, Tanamil. I had to say it. Give them all mud pies or buttons—I don't care—but make them something, please!"

Duck, who was standing by, burst out laughing. "Come on," he said. "Let's make mud pies."

"Later," said Tanamil. He was very worried. "Hern," he said, "I went down the River last night and saw Kankredin. There was no way I could stand against him. Don't underestimate his strength. I went away. I knew he could take me, and the One, too, through me. The same goes for you, for Duck and

Tanaqui, and for Robin most of all. You must take care."

"It's no *good* taking care anymore!" Hern said, and stormed away to talk to men about weapons.

"Well," said Tanamil, looking up the length of the falls, "we must make what defense we can. Mallard, can you make nets?"

"I made the best nets in Shelling," Duck said. Nothing will ever make Duck modest, but he does make good nets.

"These will be spellnets," said Tanamil, "as strong as we can make them."

"Let me help," I said. "I can make nets, too."

"I think you can," said Tanamil. "But only you can weave, Tanaqui. Please go and weave again, as fast as you can. And for the One's sake, leave as little out of your tale as you can. We do not know what small thing may be needed to complete the web."

So I climbed up here to the smoking spring again. Robin came with me. She and Jay arranged for my loom to be dragged up, too, and all my wools. I hope I shall have enough. And here was a strange thing. Robin had Gull with her, and the Young One. When they had placed my loom on the turf, she took out Gull to give him to me. And he crumbled to a mound of red earth in her hands.

I cried out with horror. "Robin! Has Kankredin got him?"

It is true Robin knows things. She was smiling at

the handful of earth. "Of course not," she said. "It means he's back, just as Tanamil promised. I think the same will happen to the Young One when Tanamil's unbound."

"Then why isn't Gull here?" I said.

"Hush," said Robin. She poured the earth carefully into the spreading pool of warm water and whispered so that Jay could not hear, "Don't be silly, Tanaqui. What do you think would happen to Hern's plans if Gull came along? Gull's older."

I see Robin is right. My grandfather has sent Gull somewhere else. He has done it to show me that he keeps his promises. But I long to see Gull. Duck and I have decided we shall go and find him if we win against Kandredin.

What Tanamil said so frightens me that I wonder all the time what I have left out. Should I say that I have a corn on my thumb and three blistered fingers? That my eyes ache, and my neck? Should I say how cold I have been in the mountain wind, these last two days? I have been weaving with such haste that I make mistakes. I had to unpick how I saw Kankredin and his glassy mages and weave it again because Duck and Tanamil distracted me when they came over the edge of the falls.

Robin has arranged for a tent to be pitched here and for people to bring me food. I think she left the cats here, too, hoping they would amuse me. But they *will* play with what is left of my yarn and with the shuttles and bobbins. I have had to ask Jay to take them to the camp.

Except when he did that, Jay has stood guard here the whole time. He is not courting Robin anymore. He has seen her with Tanamil, and he looks at her regretfully. But he talks cheerfully enough. "A man with one arm is not much good for fighting," he said, not, I think, altogether truthfully. "I shall stay here and make your last defense, my young witch."

"I don't think I am a witch," I said.

Jay said, "What do witches do if they don't weave spells?"

He is standing on the edge of the green turf at the moment, looking intently down at the fighting. It is mostly from Jay that I get my news. Everyone else is too busy. But I must have news. It must all go in my weaving.

:‖ 8 ‖:

BEFORE I STARTED to weave again, I called my mother to ask her how I should use the bobbin of glistering yarn. Duck had the Lady. I had to call without. I called, and Mother came. She dragged herself over the edge of the falls into the warm pool beside Kars Adon's grave. When I saw how ill she was, I knew Gull was right when he said she is the River. Kankredin is killing her. She looked as ill as Robin did before Tanamil came. And she was not clear to see either. She sank down in the pool, and I could see the grass through her.

"Mother!" I said. I forgot about the bobbin.

"You mustn't worry, Tanaqui," she said. I could barely hear her. "I've wanted to go down to the sea and join your father for a long time now. Open the way for me, so that I can go."

She was fading all the time she spoke, and when she had said that, she melted from my sight entirely. Oh Mother. I do not know if she is dead or not. If it was not so urgent to weave, I would sit and cry. I feel as I did when I was small and fell in the River in the Spring flood. Before my father could pull me out, I had been rolled against the Shelling jetty nine or ten times. It is blow after blow.

Jay looked at me curiously as I called to my mother, but he said nothing.

I have not had the heart to tell Duck that the Lady in his shirt may be nothing more than a wooden carving now. Nor have I told Hern or anyone. If Kankredin has Mother, we have no hope, but I think he has not, or we could not fight.

All this time Duck and Tanamil had everyone below pulling rushes from the lake. While they worked, he and Duck took a heap of pebbles and splashed a sign on each, so: ⌗. This is to stand for a net to hold a man's soul in, Duck says. They made the back of the pebbles sticky and shared them out. We all wear one, stuck to the front of our clothes. They are in colors according to clans. Our people, having no clans, have adopted whichever clan they feel like. Jay has taken red and blue for the Sons of Rath, the clan of Kars Adon. I wanted the same, but Duck says we must have gold, he and I and Robin and Hern, because we are royalty now. This annoys me, but everyone else says Duck is quite right. You cannot believe how much happier Tanamil's pebbles have made them.

When I think, I believe Hern regards my weaving as a consolation, like these pebbles. He is welcome to his opinion. Sometimes I think I would be happier if he were right.

When the pebbles were done, Duck and Tanamil were weaving the rushes into nets until midafternoon. I did not know, until I came to be weaving of the Riverbed. Then Tanamil, like my mother, dragged himself over the edge of the falls in strong spray and fell in the warm pool. My loom was showered. Duck followed, gray with weariness. He might have rolled back to his death if Jay had not pounced on him and caught his coat. That was when I wove wrong. Duck and Tanamil were both soaked; I have never seen Tanamil wet before. Jay dragged them out onto the turf, where Duck lay whimpering and Tanamil rolled on his back with his chest heaving and seemed barely alive.

"What's wrong with them?" I said.

"It's those nets they've been making," Jay said. "They've put all their virtue into them, by the looks of it."

I have conquered my fear of heights and looked at the nets. They are frail and narrow as ladders, except for the great net spread at the bottom, which is hidden in spray from here. I hear there is another, larger one, farther along the gorge of blue pools, too. The nets I have seen stretch across the falls from side to side, wherever there is a ledge or foothold. Hern has posted his fighters on the ledges at both sides, two groups for every net. Those who go down as reinforcements wait on the broad grass below the turf where I weave. We have made quite a path between there and Kars Adon's camp in the valley.

There is always someone coming or going over this turf, though I have little leisure to look. Someone saw Tanamil lying and fetched Robin. Robin came running.

"What have you done?" she said, on her knees in the warm water.

"Used up my strength for the moment," Tanamil panted. "Made something to put Kankredin in a form we can fight him in. Can't fight water."

"You'd no right to use Duck's strength, too," I said. I was angry about Duck, and about having to unpick my weaving, and sick at heart over Mother.

"Had to," gasped Tanamil. "Not enough of mine."

"Oh," I said. "And you call yourself a god!"

Tanamil fetched himself up onto one elbow and said, very earnestly, a very strange thing. "I never called myself that," he said. "Neither I nor any of the Undying ever made that claim. It is a claim men made for us, and that is how we came to be bound."

I told Tanamil I was sorry. I think this he said is one of the strongest threads of my weaving.

Robin made them both rest in my tent. When she came out, I thought of asking her about my bobbin of thread. I should have asked her before. Robin unrolled a length of the thread, rubbed it between her fingers, and then smelled it. "This seems to be the same stuff that the One used to be made of," she said. "Before he went into the fire that turned him gold. How it comes to be spun, I can't think—but then you can spin gold. Tanaqui, I think the One will tell you how to weave it in. Don't use it till you're sure." So I have waited. So far I am not sure.

Kankredin came that evening. When Jay told me, I left my loom and went with him to a ledge a long way below, so that I could see it and weave it in.

It is the most terrifying sight, though I am in a way used to it by now. He came in a mountain of water, standing a hundred feet tall or more. This mountain burst roaring from the valley and spread across the lake from shore to shore. I saw the trees and the stone barn go flat, like things of paper, as the skirts of the great wave took them. The wave is not transparent, or yet quite solid. It is green-black, stinking of River rottenness, with trees and beams and the greater part of a bridge, and many other things, carried along in it and glimpsed from time to time. But inside it, gleaming out through the dark water, we could see terrible shapes, staring eyes, and glances of bared teeth. I screamed as the monstrous thing came grinding through the lake. It sucked the substance of the lake into itself as it came, and left bare trickling mud behind. Many people on the ledges screamed besides me.

Hern sent messages up and down that it was only water.

Water. Oh Hern! It is the whole River, turned to evil. And only see what the River did when it flooded.

But people have come to trust Hern. "Only water," we all said, trembling.

The huge water came on. At the top it curved, and the trees and stones carried in there danced, as if it was about to bend over and break, as I saw the waves do in the sea. But it never broke. I could feel the power that held it upright. No wonder Tanamil ran away from it. The power was confident; I could feel that, too. They were almost at their journey's end, and the One would be theirs before nightfall. They raced toward the chasm of blue pools.

This was where Tanamil and Duck had spread their first net. The great wave ran in, piling behind itself to come into that narrow space, and came on the net unawares. Never have I heard a sound like that great wave breaking. It left our ears numb and our bodies weak. For the top curled before the mages could stop it, and the mass of water crashed down on the chasm. I was drenched by it, far up as I was. Logs, timbers, stones, and trees crashed down there with it. Some people were injured on the lower ledges, but none seriously.

The remaining pile of water faltered, hung, and finally withdrew into the lake with a grating and grinding of rock, where it paused, and its surface seethed with fury. It left the chasm broken wide, into a bay, and Tanamil's net broken with it. Tanamil had known that net would be broken.

"More of a trip wire, really," Jay called it.

But word came that two of the lower nets, including

the great net at the bottom, had been broken, too. Tanamil, tired as he was, dragged himself out of the tent and climbed down to mend them. As he passed me coming back with Jay, he told me he had forbidden Duck to go down, for which I was thankful.

The great wave stood seething in the lake, drawing itself higher as water ran into it from the falls. Behind it was all mud and little puddles. But before night fell, people on the lower ledges sent up word that the bodies of two mages were lying behind there among the puddles.

"They are only mortal men as we are," Hern sent word, up and down. Then he made a great pother, from ledge to ledge, to find out if there were, as he remembered, no more than forty or fifty mages. By this time even the most doubting of Heathens had realized that Kankredin cared as little for them as he did for our people. Their lords sent very humbly to say that the college of mages was always fifty. I think Hern knew this. He did it to cheer people.

It did not cheer me. I looked at that hill of water and wondered who could live in it. And then it came to me. People who dealt in men's souls were as dangerous dead as alive. I remembered how Kankredin had suddenly appeared to us, sitting in that chair, and I began to fear that Kankredin was not alive. I whispered to Tanamil about it, when he climbed wearily up from his nets.

"Yes, he is dead," said Tanamil. "No one can work with souls who is alive. All the mages pass through death. Then they clothe themselves in their spell-gowns, which are their acts of magery and their new bodies both together."

I had wondered why *hidden death* had worn his gown trailing beneath his horrible rugcoat. I sat at my loom, shaking, in the cold half dark. Two good thoughts came out of my terror. The first is that I, too, have passed through death, and I am more their equal accordingly. The other thought caused me to catch one of Robin's girls and send her down to Hern, to tell him that the way to disable a mage was to cut him out of his gown. Hern sent back to thank me. He sounded almost respectful.

If Kankredin had sent the wave on again at once, he would have destroyed us. Tanamil was climbing down to mend the nets, and I had then woven only as far as my talk with Kars Adon in his camp. I had to stop for the night then. But I could feel that Kankredin was—not uncertain; he still thinks he will win—made cautious. Something had opposed him when he least expected it. I think the nets stopped him from seeing who it was. Duck says they are meant to. So he decided to wait until we puny living creatures were exposed in our folly by day. He can work by dark, but he knows, by the same token, that we also appear mysterious and large in the night. See the way I am beginning to think like a witch! So the wave stood in the lake until dawn, and our army slept by relays on the ledges.

Robin hardly sleeps at all. She has the girls, women, and small children all organized. Some run messages.

Some carry away the wounded, and others nurse them. Others again are made into an army for a last defense.

"No," Jay wants me to say. "Not the last defense. The last but one. I'm your last defense."

It rather pleases me that the Heathen girls do not make the best soldiers. You would expect them to. The Heathen men show a toughness and courage that Jay often admires. But none of the Heathen girls is strong, and they are scared of being mannish. It is our own tough village ladies who are the army. Robin has sent Aunt Zara down to the next ledge today, armed with a spindle and a gutting knife. Aunt Zara is a match for any mage. She was always half a witch. That is why she hates me so.

And now I come at last to the battle, which has raged below me as I weave for two days now—as I weave and weave and weave. I dream of weaving when I sleep. But no one has slept much since the dawn when Kankredin moved the wave in against us.

Jay tells me that it came on slowly, observing. Kankredin may not have seen the great net hung in the boiling spray at the foot of the falls. Or perhaps he despised it, not knowing it was the work of the Undying. I could hear from here the repeated *boom*, *boom*, *boom*, as the wave reared and smashed and reared again. Duck came panting over the turf to tell me Kankredin had realized the net's purpose too late. The net broke under the wave, and the wave shattered with it. I could hear the cheering as the mages were swept floundering back into the lake. From there a good half of their captured water escaped, they say, and the River is running again as a trickle. They cannot now come against us as water. But they have amassed the rest of the wave and they use it now as a ladder to rear their onslaught up the falls.

Since midday yesterday they have been coming—as fire, as wolves, as scaly creatures with snapping mouths, and all manner of horrible things. Each mage can make himself seem several of these shapes at once, so men often strike at the false shape and leave the mage unharmed. The worst of their power is that they can come straight up the middle of the falls, where it is hard to reach them. Hern has hung ropes across to help his fighters come at them. And as each fresh batch of nightmare creatures scrambles up, men shout, "Only mortal men!" and they hack at them without fear for their souls. We have lost many men drowned.

When the mages come to the nets, they are forced to appear in their own shapes. They fear this and slash at the nets to break them. Duck and Tanamil sit, with their minds dwelling on every knot in the rushes, holding them together as long as they can. And while the mages attack the nets, Hern's army attacks them, yelling, "Cut his coat off!"

The first day we lost, besides the great net, four small ones. Hern and his people were driven to the fifth ledge. Today is worse. They are up on the ledge but one below me now. The women have gone into battle. The yelling is deadly. Uncle Kestrel is hovering on the edge of the turf, trying to watch. He is fond of

Aunt Zara, the old fool. Poor Uncle Kestrel was brought up here, shaking all over, yesterday evening.

"Those mages are too many for me," he said. "I had enough of them last winter. I'll stay here and be your last guard, Sweetrush, with Jay here." I have made him stay in front of me, with the sun at his back. I do not want to confuse his shadow with my grandfather's again.

Robin has just gone down into the fight, taking her nurses with her. Tanamil is waiting by the smoking spring to pipe me to the One. We have agreed I must sew the coat by the Riverbed. Tanamil says there will be time. Time is slow there. I have put needles and thread in my rugcoat and gone on weaving. I have not finished. I have not used my bobbin of strange thread yet. I look out, and all I can see is giddy blue landscape far below. But the sound of the fighting is terrible, and so near.

Aunt Zara has been led back up here, laughing like a madwoman. She has cut the coat off a mage. I knew she would be a match for them. She is so excited and horrified and pleased that she has spoken to me for the first time for six months.

"Right in the midst of him with the gutting knife!" she shouts. "I waited and I aimed, and I got him, right in his midst! Cut the coat off him like apple peel! And, do you know, he was rotten inside. Black and rotten! Think of that, Tanaqui!"

"Aunt Zara, I think you're marvelous," I said. I do.

I could kiss her, though I know I shall hate her again tomorrow.

The shadow of the One fell across my loom as I wove this. It is not so much a shadow as a shape of greenish light, with that bent head and nose I know so well. Out of the corner of my eye I saw Tanamil kneel and bend his head to the ground. That would have shown me who it was, even if Duck had not climbed just then over the edge of the turf. What Duck can see I have no idea, but he is shading his eyes as if against a strong light, and he looks as if he might have passed through death, like a mage.

While Duck stares, my grandfather has put a vision in my head. "Weave this, Granddaughter," he seems to say, "and use the thread I gave you. It was Cenblith's."

I saw the shadow of the One, Adon Amil, Orethan the Unbound, rise up in his steamy cave, and rise through the earth, through rock and through clouds, until he stood like a mountain, towering above us. Like this, he took the edge of the turf beside me and pulled it, as I would pull a rugcoat up round my shoulders, and he clothed himself in this and in the land that lay below. And as crumbs fall from a coat as you move it, the falls, the lake, and the green valleys beyond were spilled downward and tipped away toward the sea. With the land rolling and ruined, Kankredin and his mages were tipped, too, helplessly, until the grinding of the pulled earth grated them to powder, scattered them, and buried them. The River was tipped and spilled even after this, until it ran as a thread, which thread became a thousand streams, as many as the threads of my weaving. And the land was a new shape. Only then was my grandfather satisfied.

This vision I have woven with Cenblith's thread, knowing it will come to be. I thought the space of the vision was months, but when it was over, Duck still stared and people were in the middle of movements they had started when my grandfather's shadow fell. They are coming back onto my ledge in confusion, Robin, Hern, and all the army. Jay has his sword drawn. The mages are just below. It is time to finish my weaving and take my second coat through the River of Souls to put it upon the One. Then I will come back to see if my vision has come to pass. And if I have failed, I shall go back to the River of Souls for the third and last time.

:∥ FINAL NOTE ∥:

Spellcoats, as they are called, are mentioned frequently in folklore and legend, but these are the only two examples ever discovered. They were found in the marsh above Hannart, when the new fort was under construction on the mountain known locally as The Old Man. They are both preserved by the marsh to a wonderful degree. The colors are bright and clear, and the threads undamaged. The gold band at the hem of the second coat was slightly spoiled when a dishonest workman tried to pull the threads out, but this has now been restored.

The coats were known to be of immense antiquity, but they were not recognized for what they are straightaway. We are indebted to Earl Keril for first pointing out that the designs bear strong affinity to letters of the old script. Since

*then both coats have been carefully studied and the forego-
ing translation made.*

*The story is largely self-explanatory, but certain obscurities
in the text have been amended to avoid confusing the
reader. The following remarks may be of use to students.*

*Hern Clostisson seems unquestionably to be the same as
the legendary Kern Adon, until now thought to be first King
of Dalemark. The nameless King is not known, nor is Kars
Adon.*

*Duck/Mallard is dubiously identified with Tanamoril (the
name means "youngest brother"), the piper and magician
of many folktales. It is not known how far the tales confuse
him with Tanamil.*

*Concerning Robin, we may point to the belief that a robin
can answer the questions of those in trouble.*

*Gull seems to be the same as the Southern hero Gann,
whom the witch Cennoreth went in search of.*

*The Weaver herself has been identified with the Lake
Lady, the Fates, and with the southern cult figure of Libby
Beer, but not satisfactorily. The witch Cennoreth is the most
likely possibility. She is frequently called the Weaver of
Spells. A drawback is that, like Gann, she figures only in
stories told in the South. However, the name Cennoreth—
which is a Southern form; the (unrecorded) Northern form
would be Kanarthi—can be interpreted as River Daughter
(Cenn-oreth), although another interpretation would make
it Woman of the North (Cen-Noreth).*

*The places mentioned are harder to determine. Of several
rivers which flow northward, the most probable river is perhaps the Aden, which has a tidal wave, or bore, on occa-*

sions, known as the Credin. It flows from its rising in Long Tarn toward the Rath Estuary in Aberath, but it is hard to make the Aden fit the Weaver's description unless we postulate some major upheaval in the landscape since the days of the story. It has been calculated that her account should give the river a source somewhere above Hannart, near where the coats were found, but no river flows north from there today.

Elthorar Ansdaughter,
KEEPER OF ANTIQUITIES
AT HANNART IN NORTH DALEMARK